OPERATION HEARTBREAK

DUFF COOPER

WITH AN AFTERWORD BY
MICHAEL HOFMANN

McNally Editions

New York

McNally Editions
134 Prince St.
New York, NY 10012

ISBN: 978-1-961341-02-9
E-book: 978-1-961341-03-6

Design by Jonathan Lippincott

1   3   5   7   9   10   8   6   4   2

To the Lady Caroline Duff

CONTENTS

OPERATION
HEARTBREAK

PROLOGUE

It was a long way from the capital to the coast, and they had been obliged to leave very early in the morning. It had been cool then, but now, although it was not yet midday, the three occupants of the car were suffering from the heat.

The Military Attaché was also suffering from the wound which had incapacitated him for further active service. It still caused him, at times, acute pain. He would have thought it unmanly to say so, although it would have secured him sympathy and forbearance. He preferred to vent his misery by bullying his subordinates, being rude to his equals and insolent to his superiors. He had recently arrived at his new post, and was anxious to lose no time in becoming acquainted with his work. He therefore resented bitterly having to spend a whole hot day attending the funeral of a brother officer whom he had never liked.

The Chaplain was equally unhappy. During a residence of several years he had acquired the habits of the country, which did not include long drives over bad roads in the heat of the day. He had put on weight recently, which he regretted, but he had no wish to lose it in the way he seemed likely to do in the next few hours. He was beginning to wonder in what state his collar would be when it came to conducting the service. Not that it would matter much what he looked like or said, he reflected bitterly, as nobody except his two companions would ever see him again or understand a word he was saying.

The third occupant of the car had been looking forward to the day's outing, and was determined to enjoy it. The Assistant Military Attaché was a very young officer, whose health had caused him to be sent abroad, in the hope that he might benefit from a dry climate. He was well aware of the growing discomfort of his elders, which afforded him a good deal of amusement.

'It's getting nice and warm,' he said cheerfully, as the Chaplain for the third time mopped his brow. 'I suggest we stop somewhere and have a drink.'

The Chaplain and the Military Attaché hesitated. Each was determined to take the opposite line to the other and therefore waited for the other to speak first.

At last the Military Attaché said, 'There's nothing fit to drink in this damned country, and there aren't any decent pubs.'

The Chaplain pursed his lips. 'I think that a glass of cold water would be very refreshing.'

'As good a way of getting typhoid as any other, I suppose,' grunted the Military Attaché.

'The ordinary water in this district is singularly pure,' said the Chaplain. 'If you won't take my word for it, you can doubtless obtain mineral water.'

'Well, we should have to order something,' said the Military Attaché. 'It would hardly do if a great big British

Embassy car drew up outside one of these miserable little inns, and three full-grown men, in their best clothes, jumped out and asked for three glasses of cold water for the good of the house. Remember, these people are neutrals, and we want 'em to remain so, and not to drive the whole country into the arms of the enemy. Use your imagination, Padre, if you've got any.'

The Assistant Military Attaché felt that he could accept the argument as qualified assent. 'May I tell the chauffeur to stop at the next likely place, sir? I've got a flask of whisky in my pocket, if you'd care for a whisky-and-soda. We can easily get soda-water, and personally I like the wine of the country.'

Now, a whisky-and-soda was the one thing on earth that the Military Attaché most wanted, but all he said was: 'Very well, you can do as you wish.'

A few minutes later the three of them were sitting in the cool shade of a great tree with two bottles before them, a jug of water and a bowl of ice. The Assistant Military Attaché, who knew more of the language than either of the others, had slipped into the rôle of master of ceremonies. He first half filled the Military Attaché's glass with whisky from his flask and then poured in the mineral water. The Military Attaché saw that it was strong, but felt he needed it. He was in pain, but determined not to show it. He could sleep during the rest of the journey, and all he had to do at the end of it was to stand to attention.

The Assistant Military Attaché helped himself to wine and then, seeing that the Chaplain was gazing rather dejectedly at his glass of cold water, he leant over and poured some whisky into it, saying in reply to the feeble protest, 'Come on, Padre, you know you like it, and it will kill those awful typhoid germs that Colonel Hamilton was talking about.'

The Chaplain allowed himself to be persuaded. The Assistant Military Attaché looked at his watch.

'We're well up to time,' he said, 'and can afford to relax for at least a quarter of an hour.'

Peace came to them as they sat there, stillness after speed, shadow after sunlight. Irritation and animosity were smoothed away. The Assistant Military Attaché was sensitive to atmosphere and felt that the moment was favourable for putting questions that he had long been wanting to ask.

'It's a strange business, this funeral that we're attending,' he hazarded.

'It's much stranger than you suppose,' replied Colonel Hamilton, sipping his whisky.

'He was in your regiment, sir, wasn't he?'

'I suppose so. There's nobody else of that name in the Army List.'

'Was he only recently promoted?'

'You're thinking of the telegram I sent two days ago. As they're going to put a stone on his grave, I thought they'd better state his rank correctly. A month ago he was a captain, and one who had been passed over for promotion half a dozen times. He was out of a job, and so far as I could see had little chance of getting one. You saw the reply of the War Office to my telegram. "Rank correctly stated as major."'

'It does seem a bit mysterious.'

'It's as mysterious as be damned.'

'Could it have been that he was employed by the Secret Service?'

'No, it couldn't. I don't know much about the Secret Service, and the less you talk about it, young man, the better. I dare say they trip up occasionally, but I can't believe they could be such fools as to employ this particular fellow.'

'How about that packet that was found on the body? It was pretty decent of these people here to send it along to the Embassy without opening it.'

'How do you know they hadn't opened it?'

'The seals were intact, sir,' answered the Assistant Military Attaché confidently.

'Proves nothing,' grunted the other, 'but they'll know in London.'

'Was he a good officer, sir?'

'I never thought so. He was not a fellow of whom I thought very highly. But I suppose there was no harm in him. *De mortuis nil nisi bunkum*, or whatever the old tag is. I'm talking too much. We ought to be on the road. That damned clergyman has gone to sleep. Wake him up and get a move on.'

CHAPTER I

Nobody ever had fewer relations than Willie Maryngton.
Neither his father nor his mother had brothers or sisters,
and he himself was an only child. His mother died in giving birth to him on the 1st of January 1900, and his father,
a professional soldier, was killed at Villers-Cotterêts in September 1914. Willie's childhood was spent at the various
military stations to which his father was posted, and his
heart was given to the cavalry regiment in which his father
served. The little boy could not tell that all the glamour
which surrounded that regiment was part of the century he
had missed, and that even in the war that was coming the
cavalry was destined to play only a secondary rôle.

Willie was at a public school in 1914 when the war
broke out, and for a few days he had wild plans of running
away and joining the army as a drummer-boy. But news of
his father's death, which arrived long after the event, had a
sobering as well as a saddening effect, and he determined to
concentrate henceforth all his abilities on making himself
fit to receive a commission as early as possible. The Officers
Training Corps then became for him more attractive than

the playing-fields, and, although he had no natural bent for study, the mere name of the Army Class, when he attained to it, inspired him, so that he made up by hard work for what he lacked in ability.

His father had nominated a brother officer to act as the boy's guardian, and when he also fell, without having made any further provision for guardianship, his widow took on the responsibility of looking after Willie during the holidays. The loss of her husband, the care of her children and all the difficulties of war-time had embittered the middle-age of this in many ways admirable woman, leaving her with only one principle in life: the determination to do her duty. She was the daughter as well as the widow of an officer, and the noble ideal of service was the foundation of her character. She had three children; the eldest, Garnet, was three years older than Willie, went to a cheaper public school and was destined for the Royal Army Medical Corps. The youngest was a little girl of two who had been christened Felicity because she was born on the day when her father was promoted to the rank of major.

It was an austere household. There was little money to spare, and Mrs. Osborne, like many people by nature disinclined to spend, had enthusiastically accepted the Government's injunction to economise, and felt every time she saved a shilling a private thrill of pleasure as well as the satisfaction of performing a public duty.

Willie was no burden on the household. Both his father and his mother had had incomes of their own, and he would in due time inherit between two and three thousand pounds a year. Lawyers, whom he never saw, paid his school bills and also paid Mrs. Osborne liberally for his board and lodging in the holidays. She would render meticulous accounts of how the money was spent, and this effort at amateur book-keeping added to her cares, deepening the lines across her forehead and draining the colour from her fine eyes. Neither Willie nor the lawyers looked at the accounts she rendered, but she thought it her duty to render them, and whatever was her duty she would do. For duty was the watchword of this small house, situated between Aldershot and Camberley, and the only problem that could ever arise was to know where duty lay. That once known, the rest was simple.

There was, however, one member of the household to whom neither habits of austerity nor the call of duty made any appeal. If it be true that the criminal classes are largely recruited from the children of clergymen, it is equally easy to discover recalcitrants to the military tradition in officers' families, and even to find the sons of generals in the ranks of the pacifists. Horatio, Mrs. Osborne's second son, was nothing so serious, or so foolish, as a pacifist. He was one of those fortunate people to whom this world seems a vast park of amusement, and who dislike nobody except those who are bent on preventing others from enjoying themselves. To this disagreeable category soldiers, it seemed to Horry, evidently belonged. As a child he had hung about the barrack square and had heard the way in which non-commissioned officers spoke to private soldiers, and he hadn't liked it. He had seen the delinquents paraded for appearance before officers, when they must answer for the crimes of idleness, dirty buttons, unpunctuality, insobriety or absence without leave, and he had felt that those were his friends. He had once heard a drill-sergeant shout at a recruit, 'Take that smile off your face,' and the incident had made a deep impression on his childish mind. In later years he used to quote it to justify his hatred of militarism, saying that any system which discouraged smiling ought to be damned. There was nothing revolutionary in Horry's attitude; he only felt that soldiers, like schoolmasters—no doubt very good fellows in their way—were the natural enemies of those who, like himself, wanted to have fun.

Horry was younger than Garnet and older than Willie, who liked and looked up to both of them, with the respect that boys feel for immediate seniors. And they liked him. Everybody did. They were also, although he was quite unaware of it, impressed by the wealth that was coming to him, and the independence that it would bring. Garnet felt vaguely that a rich friend might be useful to him in his career. Horry thought what a good time Willie ought to have with his money, and hoped that he might sometimes be allowed to share in it.

Willie was distressed that Garnet should have chosen to go into the R.A.M.C. What he found difficult to understand was why such a big and powerful fellow as Garnet, bigger and more powerful than he would ever be, one who played football for his school and had won boxing competitions, should join a branch of the Service that was not actually engaged in fighting.

'I must say,' he said one day to Garnet, greatly daring, 'that I shouldn't care for your job—stuck somewhere well behind the lines, cutting people's legs off, with the supply of anaesthetics always running out.'

It was difficult to provoke Garnet. Conscious of his own strength and satisfied with his own wisdom, he could take as much teasing as a large St. Bernard dog. He looked at Willie with mild contempt.

'Stuck well behind the lines!' he echoed. 'That's all you know about it. Perhaps you'll be surprised to learn that the only man in the Army who has won two Victoria Crosses is a Medical Officer.'

This came as news to Willie, but he wouldn't own it, although he felt that the bottom had been knocked out of his argument.

'Yes,' he said, a little flustered, 'but decorations are all a matter of luck,' quoting something he had heard his father say more than once. 'All I meant was'—changing his ground—'that the medical profession is one thing and the military profession another, and I'd rather go in whole-heartedly for one or the other.'

'Would you indeed?' replied Garnet calmly. 'Well, I prefer to go in whole-heartedly for both.'

This seemed to end the conversation, but Garnet, seeing that Willie had nothing more to say and was feeling snubbed, crushed and crestfallen, went on, out of the kindness of his heart:

'And you see, my boy, one has got to think of the future. A day comes when the Army doesn't want you any more. They turn you out in the cold with a pension which you can't live on if you've got a wife and brats. It'll be all right for you, no doubt, because you've got a bit of money of your own. But lots of chaps find themselves right up against it and don't know where to turn for a living. An officer of the R.A.M.C., on the other hand, is a member of a great profession which he has been practising all his life. He has had lots of experience, tried all sorts of climates and had a jolly good time. Then he buys a practice in some nice part of the country and settles down to a happy old age, while his pals, who've never been taught to do anything but fight the enemy, are trying to become secretaries of golf clubs, and when they succeed they add up the accounts wrong and go to prison for peculation.'

This was a long speech for Garnet, but it was a matter to which he had devoted much thought. While Willie was still considering the new possibility of being obliged to leave the Army before he wanted to—he had hitherto believed that soldiers remained soldiers until they died—Garnet went on:

'And you know, Willie, my grandfather was in the R.A.M.C., which is another reason for joining it—and a jolly good one, too. I've heard tell that he was one of the most popular officers in India. He was known all over the country. They called him the Deliverer of Bengal.'

Garnet laughed.

Willie laughed, too, but he didn't know why. The nickname given to Garnet's grandfather sounded very splendid to Willie—like the title of a novel by G. A. Henty. But it must be funny if Garnet laughed, for he did not laugh easily. Willie wondered whether it were something improper. Things usually were if he didn't understand them, but Garnet, unlike Horry, was not amused by impropriety.

Willie took his problems to the latter for solution. The gynaecological joke was explained, but Willie didn't think it funny, and when he asked what Horry meant to do if he had to leave the Army before he was a very old man, Horry answered:

'See here, little Willie' (an unkind nickname in those days, for it meant to the British public the German Crown Prince), 'the Army's problem about me is not how long they are going to keep me, but how they are going to get me into their clutches. That's what's worrying the War Office and keeping General French awake at night. They'll have to make this war last as long as the siege of Troy if they hope to get Horry Osborne into the ranks.'

'Into the ranks!' exclaimed Willie. 'But don't you want to be an officer?'

'No, I do not,' said Horry.

'But what else can one be,' asked Willie, 'except a barrister, or go into the Diplomatic Service? Surely you wouldn't be a doctor or a clergyman?'

'There are more professions in heaven and earth, little Willie,' said Horry, looking very profound, 'than are dreamt of in your philosophy.'

So Willie's conversation with Horry ended, as had his conversation with Garnet, with a remark that he couldn't understand.

CHAPTER II

The war went on and the boys grew up. Willie passed into Sandhurst at the earliest opportunity. His arrival there in August 1917 coincided with a prolongation of the course, which had formerly lasted nine months, and in future was to last a year. This was a cruel blow to him. It meant three further months away from the front. He had seriously thought of going through a course in a temporary officers' training corps, which would have lasted only four or six months. But it might have prevented him from getting a regular commission after the war, and the thought that his father had been at Sandhurst had clinched his decision, which he now regretted.

He did not distinguish himself at Sandhurst except by hard work and devotion to duty. He had hitherto had very little opportunity of riding, which he now took to with enthusiasm. He was not, and never became, a fine horseman, but he knew no fear, and the frequency of his falls became a legend. These, combined with his keen enjoyment of work and play, his easy good-nature and his guileless modesty, made him one of the most popular cadets of his year. The fact that he had plenty of money and no hesitation in spending it may have added a little gilding to his genuine charm.

He enjoyed that year. There are few more precious moments than those in which a boy feels for the first time the independence of manhood, when he can take decisions for himself, has no longer to ask permission or account for every action.

One anxiety only marred his happiness, and even made it difficult for him sometimes to share sincerely in the alternate rejoicing and gloom of his companions. When, in the autumn of 1917, orders were given for the church-bells to be rung in celebration of a British victory they brought no message of cheerfulness to Willie's heart, and when, in the following spring, the French and British armies were driven back, until it seemed that the retreat might turn into a rout, he could not suppress a secret thrill of satisfaction. That England could lose the war was not a possibility that ever entered into his calculations. When one of his companions suggested that this might happen he was not even angry, but looked upon that cadet ever after with indulgent pity, as someone who was not in possession of all his wits.

What Willie feared was not defeat but that the war should end before he crossed the Channel. It was not unnatural. During the four most formative years of his life he had had only one ambition. To go into battle with his regiment had been for him the summit of human desire. That regiment had seen comparatively little active service during the previous half-century. Willie had read its history again and again. Perhaps another fifty years would pass without a great war. He had seen somewhere a book called *The War to End War.* The title had sent a shiver of horror down his spine. And he had heard with deep dismay people talking about a League of Nations, which would make war impossible. So all the news that seemed good to others seemed bad to him, and whatever brought hope to most of the world brought him despair.

At the end of the following summer Willie left Sandhurst. He had acquitted himself with credit there, if without distinction, and he had made many friends. It was a proud day when he received his commission, and an anxious one when he presented himself to his regiment. Friends of his father ensured him a good reception among the senior officers; and among the junior ones he already had friends of his own.

The regiment had suffered casualties during the enemy offensive in the spring. There was a shortage of officers in France and every reason to suppose that Willie would find his way there within two or three months. Such leisure as he had from training was therefore devoted to the purchase of kit. No bride ever selected her trousseau with greater care and delight than Willie devoted to the buying of the drab little articles that compose an officer's kit. He never tired of consulting those with experience of such matters concerning the latest gadgets, and he was interested in the smallest details of such objects, from periscopes to writing-pads.

If only the news from the front had been less favourable he would have been the happiest of men. But he consoled himself with the thought—a thought which depressed so many others that it was only the swing of the pendulum, that pendulum which had swung so often and so far since August 1914. There had been similar waves of optimism, like that which had followed the Battle of Cambrai only a year ago, when many had prophesied that the war would be over by Christmas, only to find that six months later the Allies were seriously thinking of abandoning Paris, and pessimists whispered that the war was lost.

These hopes and fears were for a while expelled by the exultation with which he received orders to be ready to go to France with the next draft. Earlier in the war officers had been granted a week or more 'draft leave' before going overseas. This had now been abolished, but there were few if any duties imposed on those who were awaiting departure. Farewells to relatives—a tiresome obligation or a trying ordeal—filled the time of most young men in these circumstances. But no such obligation or ordeal awaited Willie. So that these were idle, happy and proud days for him. He frequented the military club to which he now belonged, and could not suppress a little swagger when he informed his acquaintances that he might be off 'any day now.' The departure of the draft was twice postponed, to his extreme annoyance, but at last the day was fixed, and Willie, who had promised to spend his last Saturday to Monday at Mrs. Osborne's, travelled down to Camberley on November 9th.

Horry was there on his arrival and greeted him with a cheer.

'Hail, little Willie. Come and kiss me. The war's over, and we're both safe.'

'What rot you talk!' said Willie angrily. 'I rang up barracks before I left. They had heard nothing. Everything was proceeding according to plan, and the draft is leaving on Wednesday. Instructions from the War Office were to carry on.'

'Oh, I don't suppose your rotten old barracks has heard anything, nor the War Office either. It took them about a year to know the war had started, and they'll go on fighting it for a year after it's over, but everybody outside the War Office has heard that the Kaiser's chucked his hand in.'

'You think you're very clever, Horry,' said Willie, who was now flushed and heated, 'but there was an officer at the club this morning, an old officer of my regiment, who did frightfully well in the Matabele war, and he's always been right about this war—Colonel Wright his name is, and he says the Kaiser's abdication will only make the Germans fight more doggedly, and he can speak German, and he thinks the Kaiser had only been a hindrance to Ludendorff and it's probably the German General Staff that have made him get out.'

'All right, Willie,' said Horry, seeing how deeply the other was feeling. 'Three cheers for Colonel Wright, but I hope the old bastard's wrong this time. We'll drink his health in a glass of sherry, if Mum's got one, and hope for the worst.'

Willie's wrath, which always went as quickly as it came, evaporated before Horry's smile, and at that moment Mrs. Osborne came into the room. She kissed the two boys with unusual warmth, and Willie noticed with surprise that there was colour in her cheeks and that her eyes were shining as they had not shone for four long years.

When Horry asked if there was any sherry in the house, she said that she had bought a bottle that afternoon and two bottles of claret.

'You'll be surprised,' she added, for she saw they were, neither of them ever having seen her drink anything but water, or spend a shilling on the smallest luxury—'but Garnet may be coming tonight or tomorrow, and it will be the first family reunion we've had for so long.'

Willie felt that he was not to be the hero of the evening, as he had expected, and he vaguely resented it. Knowing Mrs. Osborne's economy, he had taken his precautions, and he said, as gaily as he could:

'It's not only a family reunion, it's also the orphan's good-bye. I'm off to the war on Wednesday, and I've brought some champagne for you all to drink my health.'

Mrs. Osborne gave him a quick look, and the light in her eyes went out for a moment.

'It was very sweet of you, Willie, to think of it,' she said quietly. 'We shall be very happy to drink your health, and happier still to think that the war is probably not going on much longer.'

'Don't be too sure of that,' said Willie, adding rather pompously, 'There are, if I may say so, two schools of thought on the subject.'

'One headed by Colonel Wright and the other by Colonel Wrong,' sang Horry as he poured out the sherry.

Sunday was a day of rumours. There was nothing definite in the one newspaper which came to the house. Horry walked into Camberley while Willie played with Felicity, a beautiful, large-eyed, quiet child. Garnet arrived in the afternoon. He was careful not to commit himself, but said that there was no doubt at all that the Kaiser had abdicated and that the German delegates had gone to meet Foch in order to discuss the terms of an armistice.

'After all,' said Willie, 'an armistice doesn't necessarily mean peace. It's only a kind of an *entr'acte*.'

'Quite,' said Garnet, 'but once the troops have stopped fighting I think it'll be very difficult to persuade them to begin again.'

They drank champagne that evening, to which none of them was accustomed, and under its reassuring influence Mrs. Osborne lost her last fears that the war might continue, and Willie forgot his anxiety lest it should stop. Horry was in wonderful form, or at least they all thought he was, and they sat up later than they had ever done in that house.

Willie overslept the next morning, and when he came down found the dining-room empty. Mrs. Osborne was attending to household duties. Garnet and Horry had walked into the village to collect the news. Willie felt deeply depressed. Disconsolately he consumed the tepid remains of breakfast and strolled into the sitting-room, where he found Felicity engrossed in some obscure game with two battered dolls. She took no notice of him. He walked up and down for a minute or two and then he cried out:

'Oh, Felicity, I'm so unhappy.'

She turned and looked at him very gravely. Then she nodded her head slowly and said:

'Yes, and I'm unhappy because you are.'

The front door was opened and slammed to with a bang. The two young men dashed into the room. Mrs. Osborne followed them, breathless.

'It's all over!' shouted Horry. 'No more doubts or rumours. Official announcement. The armistice will be signed this morning at 11 a.m.'

'That is to say,' added Garnet, looking at his wrist-watch, 'in exactly forty-three minutes from now.'

Mrs. Osborne's eyes were damp as she stretched out her hands and caught both her sons by an arm. Then she looked at Willie, and saw that his face was white and his lips were quivering.

'Run upstairs, Willie dear,' she said quickly, 'and see if I left my spectacles in your room.'

Willie was through the door, up the stairs and into his room in a flash. He locked the door, threw himself on the bed and burst into tears.

As he lay there sobbing, two superficial sentiments almost made him forget his deeper sorrow. The first of these was shame that he, a grown man, holding the King's Commission, should have broken down and cried as he had never cried since he could remember. The other sentiment was one of profound gratitude to Mrs. Osborne, gratitude that made him love her, for having saved him from disgracing himself before the others. One could see that she was a soldier's daughter, he thought, by the rapidity with which she had appreciated the situation and given the right word of command. That was how he must act if ever he found himself in a critical situation in the war, and then he remembered again, with a fresh pang, that the war was over. But he could not lie there all day blubbing like a baby. It was nearly eleven o'clock. He must go downstairs and show a brave face, not a tear-stained one, if he could help it.

Having bathed his eyes and brushed his hair, he went downstairs, hearing the hall clock strike eleven as he went. He found them in the dining-room, where Horry was too busy struggling with the recalcitrant cork of a champagne bottle to pay any undue attention to his entry. The cork came out, followed by some of the contents of the bottle, which flowed over the table-cloth. Horry mopped up the spilt wine with his fingers, which he then rubbed behind his ears, explaining to his surprised companions that this was for luck. Then he filled the four glasses.

'Here, Willie,' he said, 'have a glass of your own champagne, and as you won't like to drink to peace, let's drink to the next war.'

'No,' said Mrs. Osborne; 'that would be wicked. Let us drink to the British Army,' which they did, she adding softly to herself as the glass touched her lips, 'Alive and dead.'

'We've forgotten Felicity,' cried Horry. 'If she never drinks champagne again in her life she must have some today.'

They found her in the next room, still absorbed in her play. Horry filled a liqueur glass and told her she must drink it all for luck. She obeyed solemnly, and when asked if she liked it, she felt that the occasion called for something special, so she brought out an expression of Horry's.

'Yes,' she said, 'damned good.'

When the young men shouted with laughter, her large dark eyes sparkled with success and mischief.

That afternoon Horry accompanied Willie to London. The sorrows of youth, like the sorrows of childhood, although they may leave deep wounds and lasting scars, can be quickly, if only temporarily, banished by other distractions. Among the crowds that thronged the streets that day, waving flags and cheering vociferously, there were few who waved more enthusiastically or cheered louder than Willie, who had felt a few hours earlier that there was nothing left to live for on earth.

By dinner-time they were both exhausted, and Horry said that if Willie would pay the bill he would take him to the best restaurant in London. Willie didn't mind what he paid, so they dined at Ornano's, which did seem to Willie a very wonderful place indeed, and he was glad to notice that even some of Horry's self-assurance deserted him when the urbane head-waiter of historic fame approached them with the menu. His attentions were mainly owing to the fact that the restaurant was almost empty, for they were dining at an unfashionably early hour, and this was also why, Horry explained, none of the famous men and beautiful women, whose presence he had promised, had yet arrived. Food was bad in those days and insufficient; sugar and butter were almost unobtainable, but what was served to the young men, seated on one of the corner sofas in a dim pink light, with music gently playing, seemed to them delectable. The champagne was really good, and so was the brandy, though it had not, as they imagined, been bottled in the reign of Napoleon I.

They had had a long day and a great experience. They felt tired, but very pleasantly so. The sophisticated atmosphere of the restaurant made them feel suddenly older. The wine was able to have its soft, mellowing effect. Self-consciousness, the curse of English youth, fell from them, and they found words coming to them easily. Willie was able to pour forth all his sorrows, and the burden of them grew lighter for the telling. He even confessed that he had wept in his room that morning.

'I knew you had, old boy,' said Horry. 'We all knew, and we all thought the more of you. But don't you worry. You're not nineteen yet, and you'll be young for another twelve years. I'll bet there's another war in less time than that. You don't insist on a European war, do you? They're a damned sight too dangerous, in my opinion. You'd have much more fun smashing up the old Zulus or leading a cavalry charge against a pack of dancing Dervishes, like the 21st Lancers did at Omdurman. You see, you've got a vocation, Willie. I've always felt you had. You're a born soldier. You've never dreamt of being anything else—have you? Admit it!'

Willie, who was now enjoying himself enormously, gladly admitted it, and Horry went on:

'Now, if a man's got a vocation he always makes good. Somehow, sometime, his opportunity comes, and because it's the one thing he's been waiting for all his life, he's ready when it comes and he takes it. Your chance will come all right—and you'll take it—don't worry.'

He paused a moment and lit a cigarette, while Willie, profoundly believing all that he had said, felt as though he had already distinguished himself in a war, and tried to look modest.

'You may not believe it,' Horry went on, 'but I've got a vocation too. But mine's a secret. I don't think I can tell you because, if you have a fault, it is that you're a bit old-fashioned, and you might be shocked.'

'Oh, do tell me about your vocation, Horry,' said Willie. 'I long to hear, and I swear not to tell anybody.'

'Let's have two more brandies first,' said Horry, 'one for you, to help you bear the shock, and one for me, because I like it.'

The brandies were ordered, and they took some time to come, while Horry smoked reflectively and Willie wondered what Horry's vocation could possibly be.

'Well,' said Horry at last, speaking with deliberation as he sipped his brandy, 'it may surprise you, Willie, to learn that ever since I was ten years old I have had only one ambition in life, and that is to go on the stage.'

Willie was shocked. Had he been in a less receptive mood the shock would have been greater, but tonight everything seemed strange and new; the world had changed since yesterday. His first thought was that Horry was making fun of him, as he had so often done before.

'You're pulling my leg?' he asked hopefully.

'I never was more serious in my life,' was the reply.

'But, but,' Willie stammered, 'chaps like us can't be actors.'

'What do you mean by chaps like us?' asked Horry scornfully.

'Damn it, Horry, I mean gentlemen.' He could not have said it if he had been quite sober.

'There you are,' exclaimed Horry. 'I said you were old-fashioned. I might say you were a snob, but I know you're not. You're living in the past. Times have changed. They had changed even before the war, and they're going to change a jolly sight quicker after it. Not gentlemen, indeed! How about Sir Henry Irving and Sir Herbert Tree? And Charles Hawtrey was at Eton! And there's Gerald du Maurier, just got a commission in the Irish Guards. Since when have the Irish Guards given commissions to chaps who weren't gentlemen?'

This last argument, although the fact on which it was based was not strictly accurate, carried most weight with Willie. But he remembered hearing his father say that an officer, in a good regiment, who married an actress, would have to send in his papers. Yet it seemed to him easier for an actress to be a lady than for an actor to be a gentleman. He had heard of people's daughters going on the stage, not without parental protest, but never of their sons doing so. However, he didn't want to quarrel tonight, or even to argue. He had always been fond of Horry, but never so fond as now, so that he allowed himself to be easily converted, and soon he was discussing with animation the kind of parts in which Horry would do best.

When they left the restaurant the Strand was quiet, although sounds of revelry came from the Mall, where the mob were burning a German cannon. The two young men walked home arm in arm, feeling happy and very superior to the roisterers. Horry was taking his call at the end of a triumphant first night, and Willie was galloping across the veld, at the head of his regiment, under a hail of assegais.

CHAPTER III

The twenty-one years that passed between the two great wars seemed to many who lived through them to go quickly. The passage of time is measured by events, and when there are few events time passes unnoticed. It certainly flowed smoothly for Willie Maryngton. When he came to look back on it all, on the eve of the second world war, he was surprised to find how few events there were that stuck out in his memory.

He remembered very well leaving for the Continent two days after the Armistice. It was the journey to which he had been looking forward for years. How different it was from all that he had imagined! The thrill of war had been taken out of it, and there was nothing left but confusion, delay and discomfort. Inaccurate information awaited him at every turn. The troops were moving forward as fast as he was, and much faster than correct news of their movements travelled back.

He caught them up at last, and spent some months with the army of occupation. It was a depressing and disillusioning experience. Depressing because once again he found that the happiest hours spent by his brother officers were the least happy ones for him. These would occur at evening, in the mess, when the port was going round. Then would begin the endless discussions and reminiscences of the fighting. Sometimes these conversations were serious and even melancholy, but more often they were full of gaiety, for men remember more easily, and prefer to remember, the pleasanter incidents in their lives. The war was the great subject that they had in common, and it was inevitable that they should revert to it whenever good cheer and good-fellowship encouraged conversation. Nor could they be expected to know, or, if they had known, to care that the youngest and latest joined officer should suffer from their conversation. How often he felt that if only he had been present at one action all would have been different.

He was disappointed also in the enemy. All his youth he had pictured these formidable people as very fierce, very brutal, very evil, very brave. What he found was a herd of lumbering louts, subservient and clumsy, sometimes sullen and surly, but more often too anxious to please. Were these the same men, or any relation to those who had swept through Belgium almost to the gates of Paris in a few weeks, held up the Russian steam-roller, smashed the empire of the Czars and come near to defeating the Royal Navy in the North Sea? He could hardly believe it.

Nor was he satisfied with the spirit of his own men. He had thought to find in the regiment abroad a little less discipline, perhaps, but more enthusiasm and keenness than at home. So he had been led to expect by returning officers. But this, if it ever had been, was no longer the case. The men were restless and discontented, talking only of the return to civilian life, speculating on how soon it would come, and complaining of the delay. How could Willie at the age of nineteen understand that the morale of troops is better on the eve of battle than on the eve of demobilisation?

This first experience of being abroad with his regiment was not one upon which he looked back with any pleasure, and he was glad to return to England and to find himself quartered in a part of the country where good hunting was easily available. Horses henceforward filled his life. When he was not in the saddle he was talking or thinking about them. Those who do not know would be surprised to learn how large a part horses can come to play in the existence of a man, particularly of a young man, and above all of a young cavalry officer. In the days when horse cavalry still existed, the horse represented for such a one the centre both of his profession and of his recreation. It combined work and play. It could fill every hour of his activities during daylight, and prove an inexhaustible topic of conversation at night. Every day during the winter months, that his military duties permitted, he would hunt, his season beginning, indeed, long before winter with the first morning's cub-hunting. Point-to-points and steeplechases were the only other amusements in which he indulged. He bought a few jumpers and rode them in races with varying success but with unvarying enthusiasm, and he shocked himself once by saying in the heat of an argument that he would rather win the Grand National on his own horse than be awarded the Victoria Cross. He retracted this wild statement immediately, apologised and said that he must be drunk. But he wasn't, and there were those among his audience who agreed with him, to such a point can hippolatry stir the imaginations of young men.

The coming of spring meant for Willie the opening of flat racing, which in his opinion was an inferior sport. It meant also polo and the London season.

In the nineteen-twenties London was a gay city and England was a happy land. Those who had lived before the war made unfavourable comparisons with the past, but to the new generation, without previous experience, life as it was seemed agreeable enough. There had been a redistribution of wealth, but there was still plenty of it, and there was a boom of prosperity. The number of war casualties had been greater than ever before, but they were soon forgotten by the majority of the survivors, and the spectre of war was banished from men's minds.

All that the country had to offer in the way of enjoyment was laid before a young subaltern in a good regiment with an agreeable appearance and ample means. Willie helped himself generously to the good things that were offered him, but he did not fall into excess. Although he had no parents to guide him, their place was taken by the regiment, which he loved and honoured more than anything else in the world, and which therefore exercised over his conduct as strong an influence as any parents could have done. There were certain things which officers in that regiment did not do, and those things would never be done by Willie Maryngton.

He danced, he rode, he went racing and indulged in all the pleasures that became his age and circumstances. He was fond of dancing, but, out of the ballroom, he spent little of his time with girls. He found them difficult to talk to, and the regiment disapproved of men who were always hanging round women's petticoats.

He took a flat in Jermyn Street and joined another club, to which his father had belonged, and where the atmosphere was very different from that of the military club to which he belonged already. Most of the members were older men, but, although at first he was intimidated, he soon made many friends among them, for towards his elders he bore himself with a frank, unassuming manliness that quickly won for him sympathy and goodwill.

During these years, although it may be said that he had found his place in the world and was occupying it with confidence, he never forgot what he had missed, or ceased to regret it. A chance question from a neighbour at a dinner-party, 'Where were you in the war?' a chance remark from an old member in the club, 'You young fellows who've been through the war,' would bring back a pang of the anguish he had felt when he was first told of the Armistice. And now that he was beginning to meet, as grown men, those who had been still at school on that day, he felt that they also had an advantage over him.

Hunting in the winter, polo in the summer and racing all the year round demanded an income larger than Willie's, and although he was not extravagant he came gradually to understand, as the years went on, that he was living beyond his means. It therefore came to him as a relief rather than a blow when he learnt that the regiment was to go to India. He was at the time facing a financial crisis. The prospect of cutting down his hunters, and perhaps having to give up polo altogether, was not a pleasant one. The news brought down upon him his creditors like a swarm of locusts. He was horrified to discover how much he owed. London tradesmen are very patient with rich young officers in good regiments, but their patience comes abruptly to an end when there is any question of the young gentlemen proceeding overseas for an indefinite period. Willie had to sell out capital in order to meet his liabilities, and discovered, as so many have before and since, that it is always the very worst moment to sell. Looking back on it all, Willie remembered only some very dull conversations with solicitors which had depressed him more than the knowledge that he had to face life in future on a reduced though still adequate income.

He almost lost sight of the Osbornes during these years. Mrs. Osborne wrote to him at regular intervals, giving him full information about each member of the family. Garnet was working in one of the large military hospitals; Horry, having done well at the Academy of Dramatic Art, was usually with some touring company in the provinces; Felicity was at school in Brussels. They all seemed very far away from the life that Willie was leading.

He saw Horry once before he left for India. He was having supper at the Savoy Grill with some brother officers after the theatre. Horry was there with a very pretty girl. Neither Horry nor his companion was in evening clothes, which slightly distressed Willie. But the girl was lovely, and one of his companions suggested that he should invite them both to join their party. Guilelessly Willie approached them and asked:

'Hallo, Horry! Won't you both come over and sit with us?'

'No, we certainly won't,' said Horry gruffly.

Willie was taken aback.

'Why not?' he asked.

'Because we think you'd bore us to death,' said Horry.

The girl saw the hurt look on Willie's innocent face, and gave him a charming smile of compassion, which softened the blow.

Later, when he saw the two of them leaving the restaurant, he ran after them and asked Horry to lunch with him on the following day.

'No, I won't,' said Horry, who seemed still unaccountably annoyed.

'Oh,' said Willie, 'that's too bad. I'm off to India at the end of the week, and you may never see me again.'

'You're going to India?' cried Horry. 'How was I to know? Of course I'll lunch with you tomorrow, bless you. Sorry I was cross. Name the time and place.'

Willie suggested his club. Horry demurred.

'Wouldn't a restaurant be more fun? I tell you what, let's go to Ornano's, where we dined together on Armistice night.'

And so it was agreed.

It was with mixed feelings that Willie remembered the luncheon that took place on the following day. His first impression was that Ornano's had changed. It was no longer the magic haunt where illustrious beings consumed rare dishes and precious wines. It was a distinctly second-rate restaurant frequented by the riff-raff of Fleet Street and the Strand. The head-waiter of international renown had long ago soared to higher spheres, and the clientele had deteriorated. Willie noticed a couple of bookmakers, whom he knew, drinking champagne with two buxom blondes.

He obscurely felt, although it would have been impossible for him to express the feeling in words, and he would have protested had he been charged with it, that this was a place to which he did not belong. What was worse, he felt that Horry did belong to it. Horry ordered a 'gin and it' as though he were at home, and Willie felt he was being pompous when he said he would prefer a glass of sherry.

Horry was not unaware of the impression that Willie was receiving.

'This place has gone down a bit, but I still like it. You meet all sorts here, and the grub's good; but of course it's not the place it was in the days of Luigi.'

'Why were you so cross with me last night?' asked Willie.

'It wasn't you, old boy; it was your friends. I know the type—more money than brains—stroll into the Savoy Grill half-tight and think they can pick up any girl they see there.'

'No, no,' Willie protested indignantly, 'they're not like that at all. They're very good chaps; all in my regiment. I told them I knew you, and they said couldn't we all get together and have a jolly evening.'

'Yes, and you probably told them I was on the stage, and they assumed she was, too, and they thought because she was an actress one of them might go home with her.'

Willie indignantly denied the accusation.

'Look here,' said Horry. 'Supposing they'd met another fellow in the regiment, one of their own sort, out with his sister, and supposing she'd been a pretty girl, do you think they'd have suggested joining up?'

'Yes,' said Willie, candidly, 'I think they would.'

'Well, I don't,' retorted Horry, 'and that's what made me so damned angry. Perhaps I was wrong, but you know what *esprit de corps* is—honour of the regiment and all that sort of twaddle. Well, we people on the stage feel about our profession as you do about yours, and however it may have been in the past, our morality in these days is just as good as anyone else's—better, perhaps, because we work harder. So it makes me mad with rage when people treat actresses as though they were all no better than they should be. And that was what I felt was happening last night. The girl I was with is an actress, as a matter of fact, and she happens to be an angel—happily married: her husband's playing lead in a first-rate show on tour, and she may be getting a West End job. I adore her, but I'm not in love with her. I've never even held her hand in the taxi. I kiss her on the cheek, you know, when we meet or say good-night, just as I would Mum or Felicity. So you can imagine what I feel when I think people are treating her like a tart.'

'Yes, I think I can,' said Willie, 'but really you're wrong about the brutal and licentious soldiery. None of us were tight last night, and if you had come over to our table you would have had nothing to complain of; everybody would have treated her just like a lady.'

'Just like a lady,' echoed Horry, 'but she is a lady, damn you! and much more of a lady than lots of the melancholy sisters of second-rate Army officers that I've met.'

'Oh, for heaven's sake don't get angry again,' said Willie. 'You know jolly well that I didn't mean it that way. I meant they would treat her just the same as anybody else.'

Horry recovered his good temper without difficulty, and they talked of other matters. There was no more quarrelling, but the conversation was not what it should have been between two fosterbrothers on the eve of a long separation. They clung rather desperately to family matters, both feeling conscious of the lack of other topics. There were jokes about old Garnet, speculations on Felicity's future, slight anxieties about Mrs. Osborne's health. But when these subjects were exhausted and they tried to talk of themselves, they were both conscious that there was a mutual lack of interest. They had no friends in common. Horry cared nothing about the Army and as little about horses. Willie tried valiantly to discuss the theatre, but his interest in it was limited to musical comedy and revue. He hadn't seen the plays that Horry talked of, nor even heard the names which he mentioned with the greatest respect. So that they were both secretly glad when the meal was over, although they were both sincerely sorry to say good-bye.

CHAPTER IV

The happiest years of Willie's life were those that he spent in India. He had no doubt about it, when he reviewed the past. There he was able to recapture the nineteenth century, and enjoy life as he would have enjoyed it had he been born fifty years earlier. The days of the British Raj were already numbered, but a British cavalry officer could still be gloriously unconscious of the fact. On little more than his Army pay he could live like a prince, obedient servants at his beck and call, the best of everything the country could provide at his command, a string of polo ponies in the stable, and even an occasional shot at a tiger. Willie's reduced income was wealth in India, and although sometimes, sweltering in the sunshine, he would have given much for a cold, grey day in the shires, he was on the whole as happy as it is given to mankind to be.

But, because men can never be quite happy for long, he suffered during these years from one continual source of irritation and experienced one great sorrow. The irritation came from a brother officer, who was a few years senior to him and whom he had never liked. Hamilton was his name. He was not popular in the regiment, but he was indifferent to popularity. He was extremely efficient, and he was working for the Staff College examination. His efficiency was reluctantly admired, but his professional ambitions were regarded with suspicion. The general feeling was that a man who prepared himself for the Staff College would be obliged to waste in study precious hours that might be spent in playing or practising polo.

During their stay in India Hamilton became adjutant, a position which enabled him to inflict many minor annoyances on junior officers whom he didn't like. For some reason that would be hard to discover he had never liked Willie. Perhaps it was because everybody else liked him. Perhaps he secretly envied the popularity he affected to despise.

One of the reasons why Hamilton was not liked was that he had the courage to speak openly in favour of mechanisation, that fearful fate which hung like a shadow of doom over all cavalry regiments at this period.

'I'd as soon be a chauffeur,' exclaimed Willie passionately one evening, 'as have to drive a dirty tank about and dress like a navvy.'

'Of course,' replied Hamilton blandly, 'if all you care about is wearing fancy dress, playing games on horseback, and occasionally showing off at the Military Tournament, you're perfectly right to take that view; but if you were interested in war, or ever hoped to take part in one, you'd be praying that your regiment might be mechanised before the next war comes.'

This was a cruel thing to say to Willie, and only Hamilton knew how cruel it was. Willie grew very red, then very white.

He longed to throw something or to strike a blow. With diffi-culty he controlled himself, muttered a monosyllabic expletive and stalked from the room.

The wound that had been inflicted took long to heal. Hamilton had won a Military Cross in the war and was no doubt entitled to sneer at Willie, who had seen no fighting. But Willie would wake up in the night and recall the incident. He would think of clever answers that he might have made, and groan with rage. He knew all the arguments that had ever been put forward for the retention of horse cavalry, but he had forgotten them when he needed them. Hamilton had had the best of it. He always did, he always would, because he was clever. He was a good soldier too, there was no denying it, but he couldn't really love the regiment, or be loyal to it, if he could speak of uniform as fancy dress, and if he wanted to see their horses taken away.

The misfortune that befell Willie in India was his first love affair. The opening act of this little drama was all that it should have been, and fitted perfectly into the nineteenth-century pattern of life. The heroine's father was the Colonel of an Indian Cavalry regiment—an old regiment with honourable traditions—and the father and grandfather of Colonel Summers had served in it. Daisy was a pretty girl of a very English type, who looked prettier in India than she would have done at home. She was fair and fluffy, with large blue eyes and a complexion like a wild rose, the delicacy of which had not yet been dimmed by the Indian sun, for she had only recently arrived from Europe. She had finished her education at the same school in Brussels as Felicity Osborne, and it was the discovery of this fact that first brought her together with Willie. It gave them a subject of conversation, and Willie never found it easy to discover such subjects when he was brought into contact with young ladies.

Daisy spoke with enthusiasm of Felicity. She had been the beauty of the school and the favourite of the head-mistress. Some of the girls found her proud and reserved, but she and Daisy had always got on well together, and had been the closest of friends. She was glad to talk of her school life, for with her also subjects of conversation were not always easy to find. So, at the various entertainments that the station offered—polo-matches, picnics, cocktail parties and dances—Willie came to be on the look out for Daisy and to spend with her the greater part of his time. It was a happy day when he discovered that, not only was she a friend of Felicity, but also that she took an interest in racing, and was quite well informed about the branch of that sport which he himself preferred. Endless vistas of conversation now lay before them, for the beauty of the turf as a conversational subject is that in racing, unlike art or philosophy, some important event has always just happened, or is just about to happen, and the daily Press is full of reports and speculations, which can be read and quoted.

Willie's admiration for Daisy increased rapidly and, being a simple soul, he found it difficult not to talk of what was occupying his thoughts. One evening before dinner, when the officers were smoking on the veranda and the conversation was about horses, he remarked:

'That young Miss Summers knows an awful lot about racing, both out here and at home.'

'I suppose she gets her information from Coper Caffin,' said Captain Hamilton, and there was something in his tone that Willie didn't like.

'Why, is he a pal of hers?' he asked casually.

'They're inseparable,' replied the other.

'Oh,' said Willie, 'I've never seen them together.'

Then dinner was announced.

Caffin was a captain in the regiment which Daisy's father commanded. To Willie he seemed an old man. In fact, he was barely forty. Willie was respectful to his seniors, and grateful if they were kind to him, which Caffin had always been. He had an attractive Irish brogue, and a full share of all those charming qualities that make Irishmen popular. Hamilton said of him that he was more like a stage Irishman than the genuine article. He was good looking, with light eyes and dark curly hair beginning to go grey, and he was a superb horseman.

Not only could he ride a horse, but he could sell one; and there were those who said that he was even more skilful in the latter activity than the former. Buying and selling horses certainly occupied a great deal of his time, and had earned him the nickname by which he was generally known. In the horse market honourable men accept a lower standard of integrity than elsewhere, but whether Coper Caffin always conformed even to that low standard was sometimes questioned; and there were young officers who long remembered with bitterness the deals they had done with him. Willie was not one of them. He had once bought a horse from Coper and he had paid a high price for it, but it had proved a good horse, and Willie was not one to complain of the price if he were satisfied with the purchase.

'Do you know Coper Caffin?' he asked Daisy the next time he met her.

'Oh yes,' she answered. 'He's sweet, don't you think so?'

'Sweet' was not the adjective that Willie would have chosen. 'He's not a bad chap,' he said, and added with greater conviction, 'He's jolly good on a horse.'

'Yes, he rides beautifully, doesn't he?' she agreed, and added, 'And he's always been ever so sweet to me.'

'You've known him some time, have you?'

'Oh yes, ever since I was a flapper. And he came to Brussels when I was at school there and took me out to lunch.'

'What was he doing in Brussels?' Willie asked.

'Selling horses, I suppose. He's always selling horses. He's going to leave the Army soon and set up on his own in Ireland. He's got a lovely place there.'

'Oh,' said Willie dubiously. Nothing that he had heard of him previously had led him to believe that Coper Caffin belonged to the landed gentry.

Not long after this there was a dance to which Willie got permission from Daisy's mother to escort her, together with another young lady who was staying with them. The party was well planned, it was a beautiful evening, the heat was not excessive and dancing went on until late. When they at last decided to leave, the other young lady could not be found, and after a search which caused further delay they were informed that she had left earlier with somebody else. So they drove home together, Willie at the wheel and Daisy's pretty, tired head resting gently on his shoulder. When they reached the Colonel's bungalow they got out of the car and without a word fell into one another's arms.

There was a broad seat upon the veranda, on which they prolonged their embrace. Those were moments Willie never forgot. It was the first time that he had held the yielding body of a young girl in his arms and felt soft lips pressed passionately to his.

'I think I've been in love with you for a long time,' he said, 'but I never really knew it until this evening. When did you know you were in love with me? It seems so wonderful.'

That she was in love with him he had no doubt, else she would not have kissed him.

'You are so very sweet,' was her answer, and her arms stretched out to him again.

When next they spoke he put another question.

'When shall we be married?'

Even in the dim light of very early dawn he could see she was surprised, but surely she would never have allowed him to kiss her so passionately unless she were prepared to marry him, and surely she would not have suspected him of being the kind of man who would treat a girl, a Colonel's daughter, in that way, unless he meant to make her his wife.

'Marry, marry, marry—oh, my sweet, it's very late at night to talk of marriage.' She laughed a little indulgent laugh, as though she were talking to a child. 'How do you know that you'll feel the same in the morning?'

'I'm not tight, if that's what you mean,' said Willie. 'You could see I wasn't by the way I drove the car. And as for tomorrow morning, it's that already. Look, the dawn is breaking. Could there be a better time of day to get engaged?'

Daisy was still bewildered. She was a child of her epoch, gay and shallow, not mercenary or scheming. She knew that she must get married. There were two younger sisters coming along, and two brothers at school, who were a heavy drain on the family resources, even while her father still drew full pay and lived in India. Willie, as she put it to herself, was very sweet—she had never met anyone sweeter. He was attractive, too; and yet she hesitated. He was so simple and so good—she had a curious unaccountable feeling that it would be rather a shame to marry him. She fell back on the excuse that one child gives to another.

'But what would our people say?'

'I haven't got any people,' answered Willie–'not even an aunt or an uncle. I'll come and see your father tomorrow morning—this morning, I mean. Perhaps I should have done so before I asked you. I don't see why he should object'—and he added with some embarrassment, 'I've got a little money, you know, as well as my pay.'

'Oh, Daddy won't object. He'll be thankful to get rid of me, bless his heart. But are you sure, Willie, that you really want to marry me? You haven't known me very long, and one always hears about boys who marry the Colonel's daughter in India and spend the rest of their lives regretting it. Don't you think you might come to regret it, Willie?'

But as she asked the question she moved closer into his arms, thereby dissolving any doubts that he might have had. It was almost daylight when they separated, and they were engaged to be married.

Willie remembered vividly the interview he had with Colonel Summers on the following day. Military duties occupied the earlier hours of the morning, and midday is not a suitable time in India for paying calls, so that it was about sundown when he arrived, by appointment, at the Colonel's bungalow and was ushered into his presence. He had been feeling nervous, and had vaguely wondered whether he should not stand at attention, as in the orderly-room, and apply in official terms for permission to marry the Colonel's daughter. But he was immediately put at his ease.

'Help yourself to a glass of sherry, my dear fellow, and sit you down. It's been damned hot all day, hasn't it? But there's a breeze this evening. Now tell me what I can do for you.'

Haltingly Willie told his story, confessing that he had already put the question to the young lady, and excusing himself for not having first obtained her father's consent. The Colonel did not pretend to be surprised. He had known well enough that there could be but one subject on which Lieutenant Maryngton would ask for a private talk with him. Nor did he pretend to hesitate. His wife had already given him all the information which a prudent father might demand of a prospective son-in-law.

'Well, my dear boy,' he said, 'I'll tell you frankly that, although I don't know you very well, you seem to be just the sort of young fellow whom I'd like my daughter to marry. You have my consent and my blessing, and I hope she'll make you a good wife. Let us shake hands on it, Willie.'

They shook hands and finished their sherry, half bowing towards each other and half muttering something about good luck. Lighting his pipe and leaning back in his chair, the Colonel continued:

'It's a funny thing, but you probably know Daisy better than I do. I've hardly seen her, because I've been out here most of her life. Girls are very different from what they used to be. I suppose every father has said that—especially stuffy old colonels in the Indian Army. But tell me now, does Daisy ever talk to you about anything except ball-dancing and the moving pictures?'

Willie laughed. 'Oh yes, sir; about hundreds of things. I think she's very clever. She's not highbrow, of course, but then I'm not quite what you'd call one of the intellectuals. She's awfully interested in horses, for one thing, and so am I.'

'Yes,' said the Colonel meditatively. 'I've noticed that. I've noticed that.' But he didn't seem particularly pleased about it.

That was a great evening for Willie. He was not sure afterwards whether it was he or Daisy who had let out the news. They agreed between them that it must have been her father. By dinner-time it was all over the station. Wherever he went he was congratulated, and the little bungalow which he shared with a brother officer was crowded with friends who dropped in to drink his health.

One of the earliest callers was Coper Caffin.

'It's you that have broken my heart,' he said, 'for I would have married the girl myself. But let the best man win has always been my motto. Would you not like to give your bride a lovely hack as a wedding present, for I think I know the animal?'

Willie laughed, and said he would be glad to inspect it. He thought to himself that Coper was joking. He could not really have hoped to marry Daisy. He was old enough to be her father.

Of the months that followed Willie's recollection was faint and hazy. He was very happy, and the days slipped quickly away. He wrote his good news to Mrs. Osborne and asked her to tell the others whose addresses he no longer knew, and he also wrote to Felicity to tell her that he was going to marry one of her school friends, and that they often talked of her together and looked forward to seeing her when they came home. Mrs. Osborne sent him her congratulations, together with much family news, and a silver flask that had belonged to her husband. He received no reply from Felicity.

To buy a suitable engagement ring he made a journey to Calcutta, which he thought the most horrible place he had ever seen. Yet many of his friends said they had great fun there, and arranged short visits as often as they could. Daisy was pleased with the ring, and she seemed pleased with him. They saw each other very often, and they never quarrelled. Perhaps true lovers would have warned them that this was a bad sign, for those are wrong who believe that there are more quarrels after than before marriage. It was only when he looked back upon it all afterwards that he understood there had been something missing. They danced together, and rode together, and talked about dances and horses. She refused to accept the mare that Caffin had wanted to sell him as a wedding present, although she could give no good reason for doing so. She said she had heard of a better one, and that in any case there was no hurry. In spite of this continual companionship, Willie saw afterwards that they came no closer together. They knew no more of one another's heart and mind, and even the rapturous caresses that had led to their engagement were not repeated. There never seemed to be any opportunity, or was it, as Willie sometimes thought, that Daisy deliberately avoided one? If it were so, he did not blame her, attributing reluctance, if it existed, to maiden modesty.

Of all the conversations that they had at this period he remembered only one distinctly. He had accompanied her home from a party, as on the other occasion, but this time it was in her father's car and there was a chauffeur in the front seat. None the less when they reached the bungalow she drew him into the dark shadow of the veranda, and laid her hands on his shoulders.

'Willie,' she said, 'I am very fond of you. I want you to believe that, and I want you to promise me something.'

'Of course you're fond of me, or you wouldn't be marrying me, and of course I'll promise you anything in the world,' he said lightly, pressing forward to kiss her. But she still held him back.

'No, this is something serious. I want you to promise me, because I know that if you make a promise you will keep it always.'

'Fire away,' he said.

'I want you to promise that whatever I do you will always forgive me, and will believe that even if I hurt you I was sad to do it.'

'Of course,' he answered, 'and you must promise me, too. I'm sure I'll be a rotten husband.'

'No,' she persisted. 'You have got to say "I promise that I will always forgive you, Daisy, and that even if you hurt me, I will believe that you were sad to do it."'

Solemnly he said the words, she repeating them under her breath, her hands still resting on his shoulders. When he had finished she drew him close to her and held him in a long embrace.

A few days later she ran away with Coper Caffin.

CHAPTER V

The elopement gave military circles in India something to talk about for many days. Willie was at first more astonished than hurt. Men who have been seriously wounded are often unaware of the fact at the time, being conscious merely that they have received a blow. He was not proud, and therefore his pride did not suffer, as it would have with most young men. He felt vaguely sorry for Daisy, and he felt very sorry for her father, after he had seen him.

Their interview was one that he remembered. The Colonel, who had sent for him, was standing when he came into the room.

'Mr. Maryngton,' he began almost sternly, 'I have to apologise to you for the behaviour of my daughter and of an officer under my command. It is a hard thing for a man to feel ashamed both of his family and of his regiment.'

'Oh, sir,' interrupted Willie, who was moved by the older man's suffering, and who remembered the promise that he had made, 'don't blame Daisy. She may have behaved foolishly, even wrongly, but I've forgiven her, for I know she's a good girl at heart. Captain Caffin's a rotter, but there are rotters in every regiment, and everyone knows that yours is one of the best in the Indian Army.'

'Maryngton,' said the Colonel, 'you're a good fellow, a damned good fellow. I wish you'd married her. I fear you were too good for her.' He blew his nose noisily. 'Sit down for a minute and let's have a talk.'

Willie sat down, feeling curiously at ease despite the other's embarrassment, and began to talk of how he had first heard the news and of the surprise he had felt.

'I can't blame Daisy,' he went on, 'for not marrying me if she didn't want to. In fact I think she was perfectly right. It must be wrong to marry someone you don't love. But what I can't understand is why she didn't tell me all about it. I should, of course, have agreed to call the engagement off. She knew me well enough to be sure that I wouldn't make any difficulties; and then—after an interval, of course—she could have got engaged to Caffin.'

'My poor boy!' groaned the Colonel. 'You don't understand the matter at all, nor all the wickedness of it. Caffin is a married man. He's been separated from his wife for many years, but they're not divorced and they can't be, because they're both Roman Catholics, or pretend to be.'

Willie was horrified. 'Do you mean to say they are going to live together without being married?'

The Colonel nodded.

'My God! what a swine the fellow must be,' Willie exclaimed. 'I bet Daisy never knew he was married.'

But the Colonel could not allow him even this cold comfort. 'Her mother tells me,' he said, 'that she knew perfectly well.'

Willie was neither strait-laced nor narrow-minded. Although he had lived a more chaste life than most of his contemporaries, it was due rather to lack of temperament than to high principles. He knew that many of his friends were the lovers of married women, and he thought none the worse of them, although he imagined they must feel very uncomfortable in the husband's presence. He knew that the marriage tie was looser than it used to be, and that conjugal infidelity was more easily condoned than in the past. He accepted the standards of his companions, and never worried his head about them; but young unmarried girls of his acquaintance still belonged, in his eyes, to a category set apart. Married women could do what they pleased, but that a young girl should commit adultery with a married man and bring shame on her family seemed to him an abominable thing.

It took him long to get over the shock. Perhaps it would be truer to say that he never got over it. Often he had to remind himself of the promise that he had made to Daisy. Sometimes he felt that she had obtained it under false pretences. She must have known then what she was meaning to do. He could still say to himself that he forgave her, but he could no longer have the same warm feeling towards her that he had had when he told her father so. He was afraid she must be a bad girl, after all, for she had run away with a married man, who was not only a terrible scoundrel but was also not quite a gentleman.

Willie felt that he must inform Mrs. Osborne of his misfortune and return the flask she had sent him as a wedding present. It was a difficult letter to write. Self-expression had never come easily to him, and to express himself on paper was far more difficult than to do so by word of mouth. He wrestled with his task for many days and nights, but when at last he had completed it, he felt a great relief, and in retrospect he always believed that the writing of this letter had helped him to understand his own feelings and to bear his sorrow. Too easily had he at first accepted the conventional opinion that a young man who has been jilted must be broken-hearted. Too tempting had he at moments found the obvious consolation that he had had a lucky escape. He had no desire to adopt an attitude, for he was naturally sincere, but the people who surrounded him, both men and women, were inclined to approach him on the one assumption or the other. The romantic pressed his hand and looked at him silently with sad eyes, while the worldly-wise almost gave him a congratulatory tap on the shoulder. And because he was not quite sure of his own feelings he found himself meeting the sad gaze with one equally melancholy, and responding to the congratulations by an intimation that he knew himself to be well out of a bad business.

He succeeded in telling Mrs. Osborne very simply that he was not broken-hearted, but that he was disappointed and unhappy; that he did not feel that he had had a lucky escape, but that he doubted whether his marriage to Daisy would have been a success. He had looked forward to being married and having a home of his own. He had thought it wonderful that a beautiful girl should love him, and for the first time he had had an interest in life outside horses and the regiment. But now, although he had forgiven Daisy, and was determined to retain no harsh feelings towards her, he felt sure that it was better for both of them that they had not married. This assurance comforted him, but did not make him happy. She had given him something that he had not possessed before, and now that it was gone, he missed it. He had come to look forward to life with a companion. Now the companion had vanished and he was feeling lonelier than he had felt before.

All this he succeeded in setting down in the letter which he eventually sent to Mrs. Osborne, but it took him a long time to do and, almost before the letter was dispatched, he received one from England in a handwriting that was unknown to him.

Dearest Willie,
I'm so glad you didn't marry Daisy Summers. She was not the girl for you. I never liked her.
Best love,
Felicity.

Willie had not seen Felicity since she was a child and he found it hard to believe that she was now the same age as, or perhaps a little older than, Daisy. The latter had always spoken of her as though they were great friends. This letter seemed hardly to confirm it. But Willie had noticed among Daisy's weaknesses a tendency to claim intimacy with people with whom it appeared, on closer enquiry, that she was barely acquainted. Willie had accumulated a good deal of leave by now. Curiosity aroused by this letter, the desire to see some of his foster-family again, and the growing sensation of loneliness, almost decided him to spend his leave in England, but the prospect of an extensive big-game shooting expedition, including invitations from ruling princes, proved more attractive.

He regretted this decision later. Before he set out on his expedition he received a long letter from Mrs. Osborne. It was kind and sympathetic, and Willie thought she seemed to understand him better now than she had done before. She gave him news of Garnet, whose duties had taken him to Malaya, and of Horry, who had made a success in a small but important part in the West End. Felicity was living with her in the old home, but went frequently to London, where she saw much of Horry. Mrs. Osborne was sending him back the flask and she hoped he would keep it always in memory of her. When he returned to his regiment three months later he found a letter from Horry informing him that she was dead.

CHAPTER VI

When the regiment's tour of duty in India was over and they were expecting to return home, orders came that they were to proceed to Egypt, which caused much disappointment and discontent. The general rule was that regiments spent three years in Egypt, followed by five in India, and when, owing to political complications, the regiment had been ordered direct to India, they had innocently supposed that they had escaped the first part of their exile. The War Office may overlook but it does not forget, nor was there any reason why one regiment should have more favourable treatment than others, so in the normal course of trooping the regiment went to Egypt, and spent three years there, following upon the five they had spent in India.

Willie remembered very little of what happened during his time in Egypt. He knew that he enjoyed it much less than he had enjoyed India. There was plenty of polo and plenty of racing, but both were of a more professional character. In India, or the parts of it that he had visited, the Army had seemed the centre of life, but here in Egypt it was only an adjunct. In India the subject of politics was never mentioned in the mess. Everybody knew that there was a steady move towards the diminution of British power and prestige, and everybody regretted it. But there was little to be said and nothing to be done about it. These things were controlled by politicians, who, it appeared, were all determined to destroy the British Empire and to ruin the Army. But here in Egypt politics were a common subject of conversation, and everybody seemed to know something about them. It appeared also that Lord Allenby, who was a great soldier, had been weak and had given in to the natives, whereas Lord Lloyd, who was a politician, had been strong and refused to give in. All this was very puzzling to Willie. In India he had been able to feel separated by time as well as by space from the modern world. In Egypt he was in the heart of it, and he could not feel at home there.

He thought once or twice of returning to England on leave, but always some more attractive alternative presented itself. He visited the Sudan and went on hunting trips into Kenya and Abyssinia. These he enjoyed, but he disliked Cairo and Alexandria.

It was while he was in Egypt that he completed his thirtieth year, and was promoted to the rank of captain. Neither event gave him much satisfaction. To him thirty meant middle age, and although he was pleased to be promoted, he knew that in other regiments there were still to be found subalterns who had taken part in the fighting. There were also thousands of civilians—he had often met them—who had splendid war records, and had even temporarily commanded battalions, and who now had abandoned their Army rank altogether. In the presence of such people he felt needlessly ashamed, as though he were assuming a rank to which he was not entitled.

When the time came for him to return to England he had an exaggerated idea in his own mind of the length of time he had been away. He felt that he had left as a boy and that he was coming back as an old man. He even wondered whether his friends would recognise him. It was therefore a great surprise when, on the morning after his arrival, the hall porter gave him a familiar nod when he walked into his club, and he had been there only a few minutes before an acquaintance greeted him casually with 'Hallo, Willie! Haven't seen you about for quite a while. Been abroad or something?'

A club provides a wonderful home for the lonely, and an equally convenient escape from home for those who occasionally feel the need of it. There are the faithful old servants, who are always pleased to see members and who, unlike the servants at home, have neither complaints of their conditions, nor quarrels between themselves; or, if they have, the ordinary members never hear of them. There are all the daily newspapers, and the weekly ones, which are hardly worth purchase but merit a glance. The chairs are comfortable, there is never a crowd, and refreshment is easily and instantly obtainable. But above all there is the ease of intercourse—the conversation lightly begun and as lightly broken off the moment it becomes a burden, or even threatens to become one, to either party. Nor are subjects of conversation ever lacking. The news provides them, and, for such as Willie, the racing news, above all. They are varied by those very funny stories, which spring from an inexhaustible anonymous source, and which, for some mysterious reason, are very much funnier when told in the club than anywhere else.

Willie was happy in the society of men, especially men of his own sort, and he had been in the club hardly half an hour before he felt that he had never left it. After lunching there he spent much of the afternoon trying to discover at what theatre Horry was acting and, with the help of the hallporter, he was at last successful. He bought a ticket and went there alone. The play proved to be an excellent comedy, and Willie, who had seen nothing of the sort for so long, thoroughly enjoyed it. It seemed to him that Horry, who had a good part, acted wonderfully well, and also that he had become younger and taller than Willie remembered him; but when they met afterwards he proved to have altered very little.

Willie had sent him a message saying that he would await him at the stage-door and inviting him to supper. Horry, as gay and enthusiastic as ever, threw his arms round Willie when they met, and was obviously delighted to see him.

'It couldn't be more fortunate,' he exclaimed. 'I promised to meet Felicity after the show; we shall find her at Rules, and you'll be able to swallow the majority of the family at one gulp. It's a pity Garnet's not here. He was home last year on leave, but he's gone back to the Far East, and I don't know when we shall see him again. Rules is quite close—we can walk there.'

As they walked to the restaurant Willie talked of the play and was able, in all sincerity, to say how very much he had enjoyed it and how impressed he had been by Horry's performance. Horry was very pleased. All actors, indeed all artists, are made happy by praise, and Willie's praise was so genuine and so unqualified that it would have given pleasure to one much older and more hardened than Horry.

They were therefore both happy and smiling when they arrived. A tall, dark girl got up from a corner table and came towards them. She looked from Horry to his companion at first with curiosity and then with almost instant recognition. 'It's Willie,' she said, and taking his hand kissed him on the cheek, so gracefully and so naturally that he felt no embarrassment, but a thrill of happiness.

'How clever of you to recognise me,' he said.

'You haven't changed a bit,' she answered.

'Well, you certainly have,' he told her. 'You were a little girl with a pigtail when I saw you last. And then you were always away at school. I don't think I saw you at all during the last five or six years I was in England.'

There followed, while they gave their orders, a discussion as to when exactly he had seen her last and how old she was at the time, and whether she had ever had a pigtail. Like all historical facts, these were curiously hard to establish, and Horry entered into the argument, holding strongly a view which differed from those of both the others.

'Anyhow,' said Felicity, getting bored with the discussion, 'all that matters is that I was a little child then and now I'm a grown-up woman—and you were a young man then and you're a young man still.'

'How long does one remain a young man?' asked Willie.

'Until about sixty in my profession,' said Horry, 'and then they're middle-aged for an indefinite period until they suddenly turn into grand old men.'

Felicity laughed. 'I wish the girls could do the same.'

'They damned well try to,' said Horry, and then an argument started about the ages of actresses, into which Willie could not have entered even if he had known who the people were about whom they were talking, which he could not do, as all the ladies were referred to by their christian or more intimate names. It gave him an opportunity to look at Felicity. He had felt dazzled at first. He remembered suddenly that Daisy Summers had said she was beautiful, and yet, for some reason, he had not been prepared for her to be so. He had simply not thought about it. She seemed to him more beautiful than anyone he had ever seen. Her large dark eyes, her short curling hair, the grace of her gestures, the animation of her conversation, and the simplicity of her manner, the complete lack of any coquetry or apparent eagerness to please—all that she was made an impression upon him that he found difficult to understand. He felt for a moment that he wanted to laugh out loud, and then that he wanted to go away with Horry and drink a bottle of champagne, and then again all that he desired was to remain forever where he was, watching and listening and not having to talk. For a moment he wondered whether he was drunk. It was not till afterwards, when he was alone, that he knew he had fallen in love for the first time in his life.

One cause of his happiness that evening was the way in which they both treated him as one of the family. They were plainly pleased to see him, but showed him none of the consideration that is shown to a stranger. They talked without restraint about matters of which he was ignorant and people whom he didn't know. They felt no obligation to draw him into the conversation. This gave Willie a sensation that was new to him—the sensation of being at home.

He liked Rules. It was bohemian, but there was nothing modern about it. From there they took him on to a place in Covent Garden called the Late Joys or the Players Club. Here they drank beer and ate hot sausages and watched a variety entertainment. Most of the actors and the audience seemed acquainted with one another, and everybody joined in the choruses. The songs came from the music-halls of the last century, and to Willie, who had never seen anything of the kind before, everything seemed perfect. It was late when the brother and sister dropped him at Jermyn Street, where he had luckily found vacant the flat he had lived in before. They were both bound towards Chelsea.

'How about lunch tomorrow?' he asked Felicity.

'I can't tomorrow, Willie dear.'

'May I ring you up in the morning?'

'There's no telephone where I'm staying, but we'll meet soon.'

'And you, Horry?'

'I've got a matinée tomorrow, but you've got my telephone number. Give me a ring whenever you like and we'll fix up something. Good night, old Willie.'

'Good night.'

Willie felt a little sad that nothing had been arranged for the next day, but it was such a small regret that it could not cast a shadow over the great happiness in which he fell asleep that night.

CHAPTER VII

In spite of many efforts, Willie failed to see Felicity again
before he left London. He heard that she had gone to
Brighton, and he was obliged to join his regiment in a
remote part of the country. On the next occasion that he
came to London she was still away, but he saw as much
as he could of Horry, and turned the conversation in her
direction as often as possible. He felt that, although he had
known her so long, he knew her so little. He had no idea
of who her friends might be, or how her life was spent, and
he wanted most eagerly to find out.

He found Horry surprisingly unhelpful. He was, like
many in his profession, extremely self-centred. Warm-
hearted, sociable and very generous, he was always glad—
unaffectedly glad—to see his friends, but never thought
of them when he did not see them. He felt the same with
regard to his sister. He was perhaps fonder of her than he
was of anyone. There was nothing that he would not have
done for her had she asked him. But when she was absent
he never thought of her, and even when she was present he
never questioned her about her plans or prospects.

'But what is her life?' asked Willie. 'Who looks after her and takes her to parties?'

Horry could not have looked vaguer if he had been asked to solve a problem in algebra. These were questions that he had never asked himself.

'Well, you see,' he said with much hesitation, 'she was grown up before Mum died, and I think she used to go to gloomy parties in Aldershot and round about. Then people, friends of Mum, would ask her to stay in London. Then she got keen on acting and went to the Academy of Dramatic Art. Then she got a small part in some half-amateur, high-brow show, which led nowhere. She's got lots of friends, and she always seems perfectly happy.' This he said almost defensively.

'But how about money?'

Horry's face cleared. Here was a question he could answer.

'Oh, she's all right for money. Mum left her everything that she could. Garnet was here at the time, and went into the whole thing very thoroughly. When everything was paid up and sold up and probated and executed and all the rest of it, he and I got a thousand quid each in ready, and young Felicity would have about five hundred a year safe for life in gilt-rimmed securities or whatever they're called. It's not the earth, but she won't starve, bless her heart, and if ever she wants a bit extra she's only got to ask her rich brother, the West End favourite with the big future in Hollywood.'

It was true that Horry was making a name for himself on the stage and had already appeared successfully in pictures, but it was not the financial prospects of the Osborne family in which Willie was really interested.

'How about young men and all that?' he asked, trying very hard to make the question sound casual.

'Oh, she's got plenty,' Horry answered. 'I'm always seeing her with them at restaurants. Nobody I know, though, and she doesn't introduce them.'

'What do they look like?' asked Willie.

'Not like you, Willie,' Horry laughed. 'No, not a bit. Flabby and floppy, coloured shirts and long hair, and I always hope they're going to pay the bill. Girls seem to like that sort nowadays. It puzzles me sometimes.'

Willie's feelings were mixed. Relief predominated.

'Where does she live?' was the next question.

'She's sharing rooms at present with a girl friend, while she tries to find a flat. They're devilish hard to get these days. I've just seen one that I think will do for me, in Bloomsbury, very handy for the theatre,' and then followed a long account of Horry's own future movements which interested him very much more than those of Felicity.

Before they separated, Willie made Horry promise to make a plan for his next visit to London, the date of which he already knew. Horry would get seats for a play, a popular success, which he knew that Felicity wanted to see, and Willie would take her. They would all meet for supper afterwards, when Horry would bring another girl to complete the party.

So Willie travelled north with the comfortable sensation of looking forward to a certain day. He needed comfort when he got there, for he learnt that the blow had fallen, and that the regiment was to be mechanised forthwith. To make the blow yet harder to bear there came the news that Hamilton, who had been away for two or three years, was returning as second-in-command.

It was at this time that the thought of leaving the Army first presented itself to Willie's mind, as a course that ought to be considered, and not as the abandonment of all that made life desirable. He had never taken any interest in machinery. He had never shared the interest which most of his contemporaries took in motor cars. He had found them useful for getting about and he had learnt to drive them, badly, but he had never tried to tinker with them when they went wrong. Even the little musketry and knowledge of machine-guns that a cavalry officer was obliged to master had proved a hard task for him, and he would not have liked to have had his knowledge tested.

Many of his friends who had joined when he had, and later, were now leaving the Army, and the news of mechanisation speeded up the dispersal. 'You can't teach an old dog new tricks,' one of them said to him, and the proverb, for some reason, stuck in his mind, and recurred to him as often as the possibility of leaving came up for review. But still he kept in his heart the ambition that he had had as a schoolboy and which had always remained with him. He was still young and active, and there were beginning to be rumours of war. The day might yet come when that ambition would be fulfilled and he would go into battle with his regiment.

The evening to which Willie had been looking forward arrived. Felicity came in her small car to pick him up at his club. He was standing in the window waiting for her. He felt proud to be called for by such a beautiful girl. They had a box at the theatre, which gave a sensation of comfort and intimacy. Between the acts Felicity took him to the bar, where she drank gin-and-orange, while he drank whisky-and-soda. He might not have approved of this in another girl, but she could do no wrong. He found no difficulty in talking to her. Conversation flowed easily. She told him that when she was a child he had been her hero. He trembled with pleasure, and asked her why.

'Oh, I don't know,' she said. 'I suppose because the others were brothers, and apart from them I didn't know anyone else.'

His heart sank. He asked her whom Horry would be bringing to supper.

'I expect it will be Miriam Love,' she answered. 'They've been friends for a very long time. Horry does go off the rails occasionally—and so does she, if it comes to that—but they always come together again.'

'What is she like, and what does she do?' asked Willie.

'She's very pretty. She's on the stage, but she hasn't got a part just now. She's married to a second-rate actor who does Shakespeare in the provinces.'

'Does Horry love her?'

'Yes, I think he really does.'

'Will they get married?'

'I don't think it has ever occurred to either of them. She's not divorced, so it wouldn't be possible at present. Oh, Willie, tell me about Daisy Summers. I'm so glad you didn't marry her. What happened?'

Willie told the little there was to tell, and Felicity listened sympathetically. He ended by saying how glad he had been to get her letter, and asked why she had written it.

'Oh, I don't know,' she said. 'I used often to think of you, and I was so sorry when I heard you were engaged to a girl of that sort.'

'Did you think she was a bad girl?'

'Oh no, no—only silly, ordinary, and pointless.'

They went on to the Savoy Grill, where they met Horry with Miriam Love. Willie recognised her at once as the girl who had been with Horry on that night, so many years ago, when he had invited them both to join him and his brother officers at supper. Ten years had made very little difference to her. He thought her better-looking than ever. He recalled that evening which they both remembered, and they laughed about how angry Horry had been.

'He still gets very angry about things that don't matter,' said Miriam. 'We had a terrible argument the other day about conscientious objectors. I said they ought to be shot, and that if they knew they were going to be there wouldn't be any. There aren't any in France or Germany. Horry got wild, said they were the bravest people in the country, and finally swore that if there were another war he'd be a conscientious objector himself.'

'Oh, Horry!' said Willie. 'How could you?'

'It was Miriam's fault,' said Horry. 'She's got a most irritating way of arguing. She can never keep anything in the abstract. If you say that the Chinese are very fine people, she says, "Would you like to sleep with one?" If you say no, she says, "There you are, you see," and thinks she's won the argument. If you say yes, she says, "Dirty beast!"'

It was a gay party. Everybody had plenty to say; Willie less than the others, but he did not feel out of it. When he suggested that they should go on to the Players Club it was already too late. Horry and Miriam went off together, and Willie was left with Felicity.

'Can't we go on somewhere else?' he asked.

'No,' she answered decisively. 'I'm tired. Jump into my car. I'll drop you. It's on my way.'

He knew it would be useless to argue, but although he had enjoyed every minute of the evening, he was left with a feeling of failure. He thought it a pity that girls should own cars and should drive them. Especially at night. What were taxis for, anyway? He said good night almost crossly when she left him at his flat.

During the remainder of that summer Willie saw Felicity as often as he could. She seemed to have many engagements and never told him what they were. She never introduced him to her friends and, when he asked her to, said she did not think they would amuse him.

'You mean I shouldn't amuse them,' he said.

'No,' she answered, 'but they wouldn't see your point, and you wouldn't see theirs.'

She seemed always very pleased to see him, and although he did not tell her he was in love with her, she must have known it. When the holiday season came she disappeared without warning, and he heard that she had gone to Brittany. He himself paid visits in Scotland and Ireland, shooting and fishing, and thinking as little about Felicity or about the future as he could. He had been hurt by her going away without telling him, and he thought he would be wise to forget her. He began to hope that he had succeeded in doing so.

During the winter it happened that he had to spend a Sunday evening in London. He rang up Horry, and they arranged to dine together at a little restaurant in Soho. When he arrived there Horry was waiting for him at a table for three.

'Felicity's coming,' he explained. 'I told her she hadn't been asked, but she insisted.'

While they waited Willie asked after Miriam and enquired, with assumed innocence, whether Horry still treated her only as his sister, reminding him of what he had said years ago. He was not in the least embarrassed, but answered frankly.

'No, that platonic, pedestal stuff didn't last long. It can't between normal people. Her husband, about the worst ham-actor on the stage, was unfaithful to her first, so she saw no reason why she should go on being faithful to him. She's a grand girl, and has a heart of gold. I love her.'

'Why don't you get married?' asked Willie.

'The ham-actor, who's as nasty a piece of work off the stage as on it, won't agree to a divorce. He's glad of a good excuse for not making honest women of the girls he seduces. We're very happy as we are.'

'Don't you want to have children?'

'I'm not at all sure that I do,' said Horry, and became more serious. 'I have a good time myself and I enjoy life. I'm one of the lucky ones; but I've no great admiration for this world, and I shouldn't think that I was doing anybody a very good turn by bringing them into it.'

Felicity arrived late. When the door of the restaurant was flung open Willie knew it was her, and when she walked quickly in and sat down without explanation or apology, he knew that he was more in love with her than ever. How happy he felt to be with her, and with Horry once again! How different their conversation was from that of his other friends! And how infinitely more amusing! They drank Chianti and talked until all the other diners had left, and most of the waiters. Then they drank liqueurs, until the proprietor was obliged, very reluctantly, to tell them that it was long past closing time. They took a taxi, and they dropped Horry first, and Willie insisted upon driving Felicity back to Chelsea. He threw his arms round her and kissed her passionately. She made no resistance. And when he told her that he loved her better than the whole world, and that he had never loved anyone else, she answered 'Darling.'

It was not a word that she used often. Too many of her contemporaries had robbed it of its beauty, and reduced it to the gutter by making it the commonest word in their vocabulary. But in her soft, deep voice it retained its own dark tenderness and sounded to him like a magic spell. It conveyed love and sympathy, and promised surrender.

'I've been so angry with you,' he whispered—'I've tried so hard to forget you.'

'Yes, I was afraid you were,' she answered, very low.

'Why did you make no sign?' he asked, but she answered only 'Darling.'

When they came to the house where she was staying he asked whether he might come in. 'No, my love,' she laughed gently, 'of course not. There are people there.'

'Then you must have lunch with me tomorrow, for I have to leave in the afternoon.'

'I can't tomorrow,' she said, 'but next time you're here.'

They arranged when they would meet.

'I love you so,' he said.

'I love you, too,' she answered, and then firmly slipped out of his embrace and was gone.

CHAPTER VIII

In Willie's mind marriage remained the natural and logical sequel to love. If Felicity loved him she should be prepared to marry him, and yet he could hardly believe that she would. She had ideas on every subject that were so different from the ideas of other people. Under her influence his own views had broadened and undergone a far greater development than he suspected; yet, even so, she often said things that surprised him and expressed opinions that he could not accept. But she never shocked him. Sometimes he wondered why. The true reason probably was that she was always sincere and was incapable of indecency or vulgarity.

When he asked himself why he had not mentioned marriage during that memorable drive, he knew that it would have spoilt everything, but why it would have done so he found more difficult to explain.

He thought of little else during the days that followed. Out of his deep cogitations one conclusion emerged. He was sure that she would not marry him so long as he remained in the Army. He could not ask her to follow the drum. He could not picture her passing her life with the wives of his brother officers. They were nice women, whom he liked very much, and they were just like the women she had known as a child in her mother's house, but their ideas were not her ideas, nor their world her world. So he had to choose between his love and his regiment. It was a hard choice for him to make.

One evening he found himself alone with Hamilton. He had not come to like him, but long acquaintance had induced a certain intimacy, and his advice on any matter was worth having.

'I'm thinking of chucking the Army,' Willie said suddenly. 'Would you advise me to?'

Hamilton usually addressed Willie in a tone of superficially good-natured, but occasionally malicious, banter. Asked a serious question, however, about a serious and partly military subject, he immediately became serious himself, and sought to answer it to the best of his ability.

'There's a good deal to be said on both sides,' he answered. 'I know that you don't like mechanical warfare and you are finding it difficult to adapt yourself. It has robbed you of half your interest in soldiering. Much of your duty has now become a burden to you; once it was all a pleasure. And because you don't like it you are not going to be much good at it. At the same time, you are very fond of the regiment. I know that. I think you might miss it very much if you gave it up.'

Touched by such good sense and such sympathy, Willie blurted out:

'I'm thinking of getting married.'

'Bravo!' said Hamilton. 'That solves the problem,' and then returning to his lighter tone, 'Paterfamilias has no time for regimental duties.'

'But is there going to be another war?' asked Willie. 'I just missed the last one, you know, and I couldn't bear to miss the next one.'

'I don't know whether there's going to be a war,' said Hamilton, 'but this I do know: if you leave the regiment now you'll go on the reserve of officers, and if a war comes along while you can still bear arms, you'll return to the regiment on the day of mobilisation—or a few days earlier.'

'Can I count on that?' asked Willie. 'Can I be quite certain that I shouldn't be pushed off into some other awful show, be made a Colonel of Pioneers or something?'

'You may be quite certain,' said Hamilton gravely, 'that you would rejoin the regiment as soon as war broke out. We should need every trained officer we could lay our hands on.'

'That's a great relief to me,' said Willie. 'In fact it removes the chief obstacle that stood in my way. The only other thing is that I should have liked to have got my majority before I left.'

Hamilton was silent. He had his own opinions as to Willie's qualifications for the rank of major. So after a moment or two Willie added:

'Well, I shall go on thinking it over. You won't tell anybody, will you?'

'I won't,' said Hamilton, and he didn't.

•

When Willie next met Felicity he told her that he intended to leave the Army. She was very surprised.

'Oh, Willie,' she said, 'would you be wise to do that? It seems hard to imagine you out of the Army. It's so much a part of you. Would you be happy if you gave it up?'

'I should be happy if you would marry me,' he said.

She gave him a quick look, uncertain if he were serious. She saw that he was.

'Oh, my poor love,' she cried in deep concern, 'I hope you will not think of that. I have no wish to marry. Whether I ever shall I cannot say, but certainly not now, not now. If that was why you wanted to leave the Army, pray do nothing of the sort.'

'But why should you refuse to marry me?' he persisted obstinately. 'You said you loved me a few nights ago.'

'I do love you, I do indeed. But I can never see that that has much to do with it. So few married people love each other, and so many people who aren't married do.'

'That's all cynical rot,' said Willie. 'Would you do away with marriage altogether?'

'Oh no, of course not, but I feel that it is not for me—not at present, anyway. I sometimes think that life is like a play—not a very original idea, because Shakespeare had it; but he said that each man in his time played many parts. I think most of them play only one. You're the soldier, just as Horry is the actor. I can't imagine either of you as anything else. I don't think I've been cast yet. I'm not the *jeune fille*—not the kind the audience expects, anyway—and, frankly, can you imagine me playing the married woman?'

'I don't know what I can imagine,' said Willie ruefully. 'I'm not imaginative—but I know that I'm madly in love with you and can never be happy unless you marry me.'

'Please don't say that. Never is such a terrible word. You make me feel wicked and unhappy.'

'Well what am I to do?' asked Willie.

'I suppose that if I were a nice girl I should say "Forget me," but that's the last thing I want you to do. So go on loving me, my darling Willie, and I will go on loving you. And we'll have great fun, and not be too serious, and who knows what may happen in the end?'

Willie took these last, vague words as a kind of promise. He would say to himself afterwards, 'She told me not to give up hope, but to wait.' This was not quite what Felicity had meant.

CHAPTER IX

Time passed. Willie, hoping for promotion and lacking encouragement from Felicity, continually postponed a decision about leaving the Army. But his duties grew more irksome, and his desire to be in London whenever he wished increased. The regiment had lost its place in his mind, if not in his heart. He seldom thought of it. His first thoughts were of Felicity, his second of racing, so that he lived in two worlds and, together, they sufficed to fill his time. The regiment interfered with both. So that when he received yet another disappointment with regard to promotion, and when Felicity, to console him, said that captain was a more romantic rank than major, he decided to take the plunge and, not without many final searchings of heart, sent in his papers and became his own master for the first time in his life.

He went into partnership with a friend, and set up a small training-stable under National Hunt rules, partly in order to have something to answer when people asked him what he was doing, for in those days young Englishmen were ashamed to admit that they were doing nothing, and partly in order that when he went racing he might feel that he was attending to business and not wasting his time.

Felicity was sorry when he left the Army, although she had not tried to influence him in either direction. She had been brought up in the military tradition, and although she had moved into another sphere, she retained her respect and affection for the Army. Her opinions were not influenced in any way by the people who surrounded her.

Willie met Felicity by chance one day when she was with a tall young man, whose good looks were of a kind that he found particularly irritating. In the first place they were undeniable, and in the second place the young man, although his appearance and his clothes were unconventional, was not effeminate. His hair was long, and he wore a red sweater instead of a waistcoat, but there was something in his bearing that commanded respect. Felicity introduced them and said that her friend had just come back from Spain, and was returning there shortly.

'Have you been fighting in the civil war?' asked Willie.

'One mustn't say so, but as a matter of fact I have,' the other answered.

Willie looked at him with envy. Here was a man, ten years younger than himself, perhaps, who had already taken part in war, and was continuing to do so. He surprised his friends at the club that evening by informing them that he was going off to Spain to take part in the fighting.

'On which side, Willie?' somebody asked him.

'Oh, I don't much mind about that,' he said.

'Well, you see,' it was explained to him, 'either you have to join up with the Reds, burn down the churches and rape the nuns, or else you have to fight for Hitler and Mussolini and probably take your orders from a German officer.'

'Is it as bad as that?' he asked.

'Worse, old boy. You're committing a legal offence by going there at all. Of course you'd assume a false name, but if you were caught, you being an officer on the reserve, you'd probably be cashiered. There would be headlines in the papers, and, oh golly, what a disgrace for the dear old regiment!'

Everybody knew Willie's weakness, and the theme was too good to be dropped.

'It wouldn't look well in the papers, I must say. "Cavalry Captain caught in Convent," "British officer in crack regiment wins Order of Lenin," "Captain Maryngton embraced by Hitler." It would break the poor old Colonel's heart.'

Willie thought such jokes were not amusing, but they sufficed to destroy any intention he might have had of going to Spain. For the first time it was impressed upon him that it was far more difficult for a regular soldier than for a civilian to take part in a war.

Apart from the feeling of frustration that never altogether left him, these were not unhappy years for Willie. He was always occupied. His training-stable had ups and downs, and although over a long period the downs predominated, the ups were numerous and frequent enough to make life agreeable. He loved his club. He played all games of chance and enjoyed them, and the place where he had found so warm a welcome when he came back from India seemed likely to become his home for life.

What was lacking in this very masculine existence was provided by Felicity. His devotion to her never faltered, and she provided for him all that he demanded in the region of beauty and romance. She made no demands upon him. It was he who had always to arrange their meetings, and they were not as frequent as he would have liked. Often he felt that she was treating him badly, but he had only to be with her for five minutes to forget his grievance. Sometimes weeks or even months passed without their being alone together for a moment, and she seemed to be unaware of the fact. Sometimes she seemed to welcome and give back all his passion, at others she hardly allowed him to touch her hand. When he asked her to explain, or to give any reason for such strange alterations in her behaviour, she would say that she was sorry, she knew herself to be very tiresome, but he must take her as she was.

Willie went on living in Jermyn Street, where Felicity never visited him. It was one of her own unwritten laws. Nor did he invite her. There were still matters that he could not discuss with her, and favours that he could not ask. But despite the restrictions set upon their love-making, she made him happy. Her companionship was an unending pleasure, intensified by the thrill of desire. Sometimes, in the summer, they would take picnics into the country, spreading a cloth in some green, secluded spot and sleeping afterwards under the trees. Sometimes they would go to the coast and bathe in the sea. Best of all, he thought, were the autumn and winter evenings when, having spent the day in the open air, hunting or racing, he would return to London and go to the club, where he would remain until the hall-porter came and murmured to him, confidentially, that there was a lady waiting for him outside. Then they would perhaps, if it were not too late, have something to eat and drink before going to the theatre, and afterwards they would have supper either alone or with Horry, and Horry would usually bring a fourth. It was not always Miriam, and when there was a change Willie and Felicity would enjoy, afterwards, criticising the new favourite and speculating on Horry's degree of intimacy with her. Horry was earning a large salary now, his services were always in demand and he could pick and choose his parts. He had taken his flat in Bloomsbury, of which Willie approved, because it lay in the opposite direction to Chelsea, and there could therefore never be any occasion for Horry to drive Felicity home. She, on the other hand, after all these years, was still looking for a flat, and still sharing rooms with a friend, which Willie deplored, because it disposed of any argument that he could use for crossing the threshold. It was a strange love affair, but Willie was beginning to become reconciled to it, as he was beginning to become reconciled to his existence. It seemed to be his fate, he sometimes thought, to be a soldier who never went to war, and a lover who never lay with his mistress.

CHAPTER X

While his life was thus jogging easily along there happened the great political event that was known as the Munich crisis. It made a disturbance in many people's lives. In Willie's it made a vast upheaval. Once again he felt as he had felt twenty years before and, while nearly all the world was hoping for peace, he prayed for war. Naturally he resented the settlement with great bitterness, and he was glad to find that there were others who felt as he did. His reasons were not their reasons, but this did not prevent him from applauding their denunciation of the shameful surrender. But when they said that the worst part of the policy was that it only meant we should have to fight the war later under less favourable conditions, he secretly hoped that they were right, and that it would come as soon as possible.

He was disappointed in the attitude of Felicity, who was for peace at any price, and they nearly quarrelled about it, as at that time so many good friends did. But he found an unexpected and fervent ally in Horry. It was unexpected, because he had always thought of Horry as a man who was opposed to any form of violence. He was, however, one who behind an easy-going, humorous approach to life hid a profound hatred of injustice and cruelty. He knew of the fate that had befallen some Jewish members of the German theatrical world, and he could not bear to think of Englishmen shaking the hand of the man who was responsible for such enormities. He was much more violent than Willie, and what he had to say about the paper signed by Hitler, which the Prime Minister waved triumphantly in the face of the applauding populace, was very savage.

In the days before the settlement, while Willie was eagerly awaiting his mobilisation orders, he had travelled up to where his regiment was stationed in order to be on the spot. The Colonel was abroad on leave, which shocked him, and Hamilton was in command. Hamilton refused to believe there would be a war, and told Willie not to get over-excited. He had been in Germany himself last summer and had talked to some German officers—very good chaps. He thought that if our politicians knew their business they could arrange for Germany to fight Russia. The officers he had met were pro-British, but very keen to have a go at the Reds. We ought to encourage them to do so and kill two birds with one stone.

Willie had asked whether the winner would not then turn on us, but Hamilton had replied that both sides would be exhausted.

'And then the looker-on, who will be us, and who, as usual, will have seen most of the game, who will have learnt a lot about modern warfare, without fighting, and will have built up his own armaments while the belligerents are destroying theirs, will be in a position to dictate to both sides. That's what's called statesmanship.'

'I don't care what it's called,' said Willie, 'it sounds to me a dirty, tricky, cowardly business—the sort of thing that politicians would invent—and, what's more, I don't believe that any good will come of it. Well, you will know where I am if you want me.'

'We shan't forget, Willie, and you may be sure that we shall send for you in the hour of danger.'

Willie had felt that Hamilton was laughing at him, and hated him for it, but henceforth he had a very definite object in life and a great hope in his heart.

During the months that followed he thought of nothing but the coming war. He was now thirty-nine, and he had never bothered to take care of his health. Riding had kept him active, and he had detected in himself no symptoms of growing old. But he consulted a doctor and insisted upon a thorough examination. The doctor found little wrong with him, but suggested fewer cocktails and plainer food, and Willie followed his directions as scrupulously as though they were military orders.

He saw less of Felicity during this year. She refused to take life as seriously as he did, and preferred to accept the assurances given by Ministers and newspapers that there was nothing to worry about.

CHAPTER XI

Being on the reserve of officers, Willie did a short period of training with his regiment every year, and it so happened that he was actually with the regiment and under canvas in the month of September when the war broke out. Once again he experienced the same thrill of exultation that he had known just twenty-one years before when he was warned that he was to go with the next draft to France. He felt no older than he had done then, and on his knees he thanked heaven that his chance had not come too late. In the camp during those first days everything was in a state of feverish activity, for it was known that the regiment would be among the first to go.

Then came the shattering blow. One morning the Colonel sent for him. 'I've bad news, I fear, for you, Willie, but it's bad news for me, too. We're both in the same boat, or rather we're both out of it; neither of us is to go with the first contingent. Hamilton is taking the regiment abroad, and you and I have got to stay behind, look after what's left of it, and train on the young officers.'

Willie's mouth went dry, he was unable to speak, and for one terrible moment he feared he was going to cry.

'Don't take it too hard,' the Colonel went on. 'It's worse for me than for you. In my case, if they don't let me go now it's a hundred to one they won't let me go at all. It means I'm on the shelf, finished for life.'

Willie longed to say that the Colonel had fought in the last war, as the row of ribbons on his chest bore witness, that he was over fifty, a married man with children, and that he had much to console him for staying at home. He wanted to fall on his knees and beg to be allowed to go, but he knew that the decision did not rest with the Colonel, so that he could only stand there, still unable to speak.

'Don't take it too hard, Willie,' the Colonel repeated, seeing that he was taking it very hard indeed. 'I remember so well at the beginning of the last war, when some fool in high places had said, or was reported to have said, that it would all be over by Christmas, and lots of us were in despair because we thought we should never get out in time. But we all went in the long run, and it will be just the same again—heavy casualties in the first scrap, more officers wanted, none of the new boys ready to go. They'll be grateful enough for the old 'uns then, and there won't be too many of them. Meanwhile there will be plenty of work for us to do at home, and very important work too, and there's a job or two I want you to get on with immediately.'

Willie was thankful that the Colonel then went on to explain to him a number of things that he wanted done which would necessitate a visit to the War Office and several days in London. He was, in fact, to act as second-in-command of the training unit that would remain behind. Although he found it difficult to follow all that the Colonel said, and was obliged to ask a number of questions, he was thankful to have these matters to discuss and not to be obliged to refer to the fearful blow which he had just received. If only he had been prepared for it, he felt that he could have borne it better. But in his crass stupidity, he told himself, it was the one thing that had never occurred to him. He knew perfectly well that when a regiment went abroad on active service some officers and men were left behind. But he had never thought that he would be among those officers. Some people, he told himself, were struck by lightning, some were eaten by sharks, some won the Calcutta sweepstake, but he had never believed that any of those fates would befall such an ordinary chap as him, Willie Maryington. And he would never have thought that he would be the officer who was left behind. The Colonel had talked about the first scrap, but that was just the scrap that he wanted to be in. He had said something about heavy casualties. Willie minded little how heavy they were if he was in it, but how could he bear to sit at home hoping that his brother officers would be killed, so that he could take their place?

No reference was made in the mess that evening to the regiment's forthcoming departure, but Willie felt that it was generally known that he was not to go. Everybody was polite and kind to him as though he had just suffered some domestic tragedy, and, when he said that he was going to London next morning, nobody asked why.

When Willie went into his club on the following day he was surprised to find how many of the civilian members were already in uniform, and how many were expecting to go overseas almost immediately. At the time this made his position more painful, although subsequent experience taught him that these hopes of active service, if genuine, were too optimistic, and many of the most confident remained in uniform, and in the club, for the rest of the war.

He spent the greater part of the next day at the War Office, and was very far from having completed his mission at the end of it. The light was failing as he turned up Whitehall towards Trafalgar Square. He had almost bumped into a man who was walking rapidly in the opposite direction, when he saw that he was Horry, and they greeted one another.

'You're a bit off your beat here, Horry,' he said. 'Turn back with me and we'll have a drink at the Carlton bar.'

'I'm sorry, old chap,' said Horry, 'but I'm in a hurry. Walk along with me in my direction for a bit.'

Willie turned. As he did so he glanced curiously at Horry. There was something unusual in his appearance. Could he be sunburnt? No—he looked again, and then he saw what it was.

'Horry,' he said quietly, 'have you been playing in a matinée?'

'No, indeed. My show came off last week—and who ever heard of a matinée on a Friday?'

'Then, by God, Horry, I don't understand it,' said Willie rather fiercely. 'I thought perhaps you'd forgotten to take off your make-up. Are you aware, man, that your face is painted?'

He asked the question as though it were an accusation, and in order to add solemnity to it, he stopped, laid his hand on Horry's arm and looked straight into his eyes.

Horry threw back his head with his old gay laugh. 'Oh, my beloved Willie,' he said. 'Scotland Yard's just round the corner. Would you care to run me in for accosting? Come on, you old silly. I've got no time to lose.'

'But explain, for God's sake explain,' said Willie, as they walked on.

'It's very simple,' said Horry. 'I'm over forty, you know. I never thought I looked it, but it seems I do. They've turned me down at two of these damned recruiting places already, but there's one down here near Westminster Bridge. They haven't got the electricity working in it yet, but they keep it open till six, and by then the light's pretty bad. The chaps will be tired, they don't know me as you do, so they won't suspect anything, and I believe with this make-up I'll pull it off.'

'Oh, Horry, how splendid! I thought that you'd be the last person to do a thing like this.'

'I know.' Horry looked almost ashamed of himself. 'I'm not so keen on King and Country and all that stuff, but when I think about those blasted Nazis I just feel that I can't walk on to the stage and make an ass of myself as long as one of the bastards is left alive.'

Willie was deeply moved, but all he could mutter was 'Damned good show,' and as they had reached the end of Whitehall he turned, rather abruptly, towards Storey's Gate and began walking back to his club across the park. His mind was full of admiration for Horry and of pity for himself. Here was a man two years older than he was, who, since leaving school, had never done a day's military training, and who might now be going to the war, while he, whose whole life had been devoted to the Army, who had made every possible effort to render himself an efficient officer, was forced to stay at home. The injustice of it rankled deeply.

He had broken off his conversation with Horry so suddenly that he had forgotten to ask him to telephone the result of his visit to the recruiting station. When he reached his club, therefore, he rang up and heard the jubilant-voice of Horry at the other end of the line. All had gone well. The only doubt in the minds of the officials, so he assured Willie, was whether he was old enough to join the Army. He was to report on the following day.

Willie suggested that they should dine together, but Horry, after a moment's hesitation, feared it was impossible. Willie concluded that he was having a farewell dinner with Miriam, and keenly envied him. He asked for news of Felicity. He had tried to find her by telephone without success. Horry gave him a number. When he succeeded in getting it, after some difficulty, and asked for Miss Osborne, he was informed in a harsh female voice that 'Osborne would be coming on duty at 10 p.m.' He enquired who it was that he had the honour of speaking to, and learnt that it was the Superintendent of the Chelsea Branch of the Auxiliary Fire Service. He asked that Osborne might be requested to ring up his number when she arrived, and a grudging assent was given.

He was in the middle of a rubber of bridge after dinner when the call came through. Felicity's voice sounded tired on the telephone and not very friendly. After the usual greetings she said:

'I hope you're enjoying the war that you've been looking forward to for so long.'

'Oh no, Felicity,' he answered. 'I am not enjoying it at all.'

Her voice changed at once, and the warmth he loved so much came back into it.

'My poor Willie. I hate you to be unhappy. We'll lunch together tomorrow, and you shall tell me all about it.'

She gave him the name of a restaurant in Chelsea, and told him the hour at which she would be there, warning him that her time was limited and that he must be punctual.

On the following day he waited for her at the restaurant for half an hour. Thinking there had been a mistake, he was about to leave, for it was not a restaurant which tempted him to have luncheon alone, and he was standing at the entrance, when she came running down the street. Breathlessly she explained that she had been unable to get away earlier, that her hours of duty were always being changed, that she would never have forgiven him if he hadn't waited, but that now all was well, as she was free for the afternoon.

He thought that she had never looked so lovely. The uniform—dark blue tunic and trousers and a small blue hat that could not contain her thick curling hair—became her admirably. She carried her gas mask slung over her shoulder and somehow conveyed a curious impression of efficiency. He was delighted with her.

'Tell me quickly,' he said, 'all about this Army you have joined, what your duties are and how you like it.'

'It seemed,' she said, 'the best thing to do. One can't get into the Wrens, the Ats all hate it, and I can't bear the uniform of the Waafs, so here I am. I've got some friends in the same show. We can't have much to do until the bombing starts, then we shall have to go round putting out the fires and carting away the corpses. I'm only a driver. The one thing I can do is to drive a car, but I've only just learnt to clean one. Look!' She held out to him her beautiful hands, already dirtied and roughened by labour.

He took one of them in his, pointed to the scratches on it, saying, 'Honourable scars, honourable scars,' then turned it over tenderly and kissed the palm.

'Even you,' he murmured, 'wounded already!' He asked her whether she had heard about Horry. She had heard nothing, and when he told her she was not surprised.

'I thought he'd do something like that,' she said, 'but I wish he could have had a commission. He loves his comforts, and he has been used to them for so long.'

'Perhaps he'll get one,' said Willie. 'Serve him right if he does, for then they won't let him go near the fighting.'

He poured forth all his own unhappiness, and Felicity listened with large-eyed sympathy. She offered him such consolation as she could, but found little to say that he had not said to himself already. There was, of course, the very likely possibility of heavy casualties, against which Willie argued that young officers were being rapidly trained to fill the gaps.

Felicity maintained, rather feebly, the view that this war was not going to be like the last. Not only was there just as much important work to be done at home, but the people who stayed at home would be in as great danger as those at the front.

'Not the soldiers,' said Willie bitterly. 'You ought to see our air-raid shelters; we've been digging them all the summer, although the C.O. didn't believe in war. They're the best in the country and, what's more, it's an order to go down into them at the first alert. It's an offence to risk the life of one of His Majesty's valuable soldiers, even those who are too old to go out and fight for him. And what do you suppose we're spending our time doing now?' he added. 'Camouflaging our barracks!'

'Well, you won't be safe when you come to London, anyhow, and I hope you'll come often because I see that I'm going to be terribly bored.'

'I'll come as often as I can; you can count on that. But if you think that a bomb falling on my head in a London street is going to make up to me for not fighting with the regiment in France, you're wrong.'

'My poor Willie,' said Felicity sadly. 'It seems to me that wars don't make people happy—not even the people who wanted them'—and she stretched her hand across the table and held his for a minute.

CHAPTER XII

Willie was kept very busy that winter and the time passed quickly. If there were few casualties it was some consolation to him to know that there was so little fighting, and therefore that he was not missing much. He seldom came to London, and when he did he found it difficult to see Felicity, whose time also was occupied with small, tiresome duties, and who was intensely disliking her apparently unnecessary job, which increased the dreariness of the hard winter, the black-out and the uneventful war.

The only casualty that occurred in Willie's regiment was one that he least desired. The Colonel greeted him one morning in high spirits with the information that Hamilton had suffered some injury and was coming home.

'It seems,' he said, 'that he had a fall out riding. It has lamed him, and he's coming home for a bit, and I am to take his place. He'll take over here for the time being. He's fit for light duty.'

'What was he riding a horse for?' grumbled Willie. 'Why doesn't he stick to his dirty old tank? He can't fall off that.'

That the Colonel should go out and that Hamilton should come home was a double-barrelled disaster for Willie, and made a bad beginning to the second six months of the war. Events of so much greater importance, however, followed that for a while Willie forgot his own grievances while the German armies swept through Denmark, Norway, Holland, Belgium and France. His reaction to these tremendous events was that of many Englishmen. After the dim frustration of the first eight months he felt a new enthusiasm and a kind of spiritual exaltation. For the first time in his life it occurred to him that defeat was possible, but it was a possibility that did not appal him. There could be no defeat unless the enemy landed, and if they landed there could be no defeat so long as there was one true Englishman alive. Then at last he would have the opportunity of fighting for his country and of dying for it, if need be.

On one of his visits to London at about the time of the fall of France he spent an evening with Felicity. She greeted him with the news that Horry had been killed in Boulogne. She had only just heard, but she was quite calm about it, although Willie knew that it meant even more to her than it did to him.

'Garnet told me this morning,' she said. 'He had had the telegram as being next of kin.'

'It's too bad,' said Willie.

'Too bad,' she said.

'I sometimes think,' he went on, 'that we shall all be killed. I'd sooner be, if we're going to lose the War.'

'Of course,' she said quietly. 'But it won't be so easy for women.'

'Will they let you fight?' he asked.

'Can they stop us?' she answered. 'We had a lecture yesterday about Molotov bombs. You throw them out of the window at a tank, and if you hit it the tank goes up in smoke. It sounds fun, but nobody has seen one yet.'

Then they went on to talk of Horry, of how much they had loved him and how deeply they would miss him for the rest of their lives. It was a calm, sad evening. When they parted and Willie took her in his arms and kissed her cheek, he felt they had never been so close to one another before.

The important thing for Willie at this time was that the regiment, having suffered very lightly, was home again, and that he was with it. The Colonel was no longer there. He had had the final satisfaction of commanding during the retreat to Dunkirk, and had been transferred to some non-combatant job. Hamilton had been cured of his disability, promoted to the substantive rank of lieutenant-colonel and was in command. This slightly, but only slightly, mitigated Willie's happiness in being with his comrades again. He felt that the greater part of what was left of the Army was now in England, so that he was happy to be there too, and he secretly hoped that the enemy would invade.

The Battle of Britain damped his hopes, but he was uplifted by the glory of it, and cursed his fate that he had never learned to fly. His friends consoled him with the assurance that, judging by his prowess at the wheel of a car, he would certainly have destroyed any aeroplane he was in charge of, and himself with it. And even if he had survived he would have been permanently grounded long ago.

He still had his flat in London, and he went there as often as he could. He was there on the Sunday evening in September when the first serious bombing attack took place. Felicity was on duty that night. He was able to have only a few words with her on the telephone the following morning before he travelled back. When he pressed her for some account of her experiences she was reticent.

'Come on,' he urged, 'tell me more about it. What sort of time did you have?'

'Pretty bloody,' she said, and he could get nothing more out of her, but he felt as he returned to the country that she had come closer to the war than he had.

As the days shortened and the frequency of bombing raids increased, the rumours of invasion began to be discredited, and in Willie's regiment they were replaced by whispers that the regiment would shortly be moving to the Middle East. Now, so it seemed to Willie, the great crisis of his life must come. When they had crossed the Channel without him, the blow had been severe, but they had been distant only a day's journey, or a few hours in the air, and he had always hugged to his heart the hope that any morning the summons to join them might arrive. But if they went to the Middle East, and it was said that troops now travelled round the Cape to get there—if they went to the Middle East without him, he felt that his fate would be sealed. Speculation on this subject occupied his mind day and night. Here at home he was treated like any other officer. He was senior captain and performed all the duties and received all the respect belonging to his rank. His health was excellent. He had worked conscientiously to make himself efficient. Conceit was the least of his failings, but he quite honestly believed that he was as good an officer as the majority. *But,* that terrible word which came at the end of all his optimistic reasonings, *but* he had been left behind a year ago when he was thirty-nine, he was now forty and soon he would be forty-one. The next youngest captain in the regiment was thirty-four. This captain was married with children, as so many of these young men were, while he himself was single, with no dependants in the world. That was a consideration that ought surely to be taken into account.

The men liked him—that he knew—and so did his brother officers. He was not brilliantly clever, but nor were they. He knew his job as well as they did, and had more experience. It was true that he had been away from the regiment for some years, but he had worked hard to catch up, and thought he had succeeded. Did they think that because he was a little older he was more likely to go sick? A doctor had assured him that a healthy man of forty was in every way as sound a proposition as a man of thirty. He had passed his medical examination with flying colours. Since he had rejoined he had not had a day's illness, which was more than most of them could say. But, but they had left him behind a year ago, why should they take him with them now?

Willie became so haunted by this obsession that he finally decided that he had better take some action that would put himself out of his agony. Between the decision and the action many days passed. At last one night, which was selected for no better reason than that he had had an extra glass of port after dinner, and that he found himself alone with Hamilton, the others having gone to the cinema, he boldly broached the subject.

'They say we may be going overseas again,' he began.

'Do they?' said Hamilton, stretching for a newspaper.

'Oh, I'm not trying to extract confidential information about the movement of troops. I'm only interested in the movements of Captain Maryngton. I don't want to know whether the regiment is going or not, but what I do want to know—pretty damned desperately bad I want to know—is whether, if the regiment does go, I am likely to go with it.'

Hamilton was silent.

'Look here, Colonel,' Willie went on. 'You've known me for a long time, and you must know what this thing means to me. I missed the last war by a few weeks, and all I have hoped for all my life is to see some fighting with the regiment. I had given up hope some years ago, when I left the Army. I thought there wouldn't be another war in my time, and then I thought I might get married. You were the only fellow I told, and I don't believe you ever repeated it, for which I'm damned grateful. Well, it didn't come off, and now I don't expect it ever will. I'm alone in the world, hale and hearty, just the sort of cannon-fodder they ought to be looking for—and, and, oh Hamilton, for God's sake tell me—have I got a chance?'

Hamilton replied, 'Not an earthly.'

Willie put his face in his hands, and Hamilton went on calmly:

'As you have asked me, it is better that you should know the truth. No officers, under field rank, of your age, or anything like your age, are being sent abroad. You may have heard of exceptions. There are exceptions to every rule, but I can see no chance of your being one. It's bad luck, but that's how it is.'

'I see,' said Willie, 'I see.'

He got up slowly, left the room and walked upstairs to bed. As he went he thought he might have asked whether he had any chance of promotion. But he knew what the answer would have been.

The final calamity comes often almost as a relief after long anxiety, and Willie, although he assured himself that life no longer held any interest for him, slept better that night than he had done for some time. Next morning he felt very miserable, but told himself that he must bear sorrow with fortitude, and that at such a moment in the world's history there were more important things to think about than the fate of Willie Maryngton. There was still the regiment and there was still Felicity.

In a few days came confirmation of the rumours about the regiment's movements, and it was followed by definite orders to sail. Henceforth they all lived in a turmoil of preparation, where there was as much work for Willie to do as for anyone else. His heart was in the work and he threw himself into it with passion, resisting firmly any inclination to pause and think. Like a discarded suitor employed on the preparations for the wedding of his beloved, he tried to think only of the task in hand, and to forget what must be the end of it. But too soon the end arrived. There could be none of those festivities or farewell parties that used to celebrate the departure of troops. The demands of security insisted that to the public eye the regiment should be there one day, carrying on their normal functions and giving no sign of departure, and on the morrow they should have disappeared, leaving no trace behind. Willie travelled with them to the port of embarkation, and actually went on board the ship in which they were sailing. When he had shaken hands with some of his friends, and came over the side for the last time, he had a curious and most uncomfortable feeling in his chest, and he found himself foolishly wondering whether people's hearts really do break, whether it might not be more than a mere figure of speech.

CHAPTER XIII

When he got back to London that evening an air-raid was in progress. There seemed to be one every night now. It was December 1940. There was no hope of getting a taxi at the station, so he left his kit there and walked through the deserted streets to his club. There were sounds of distant explosions, but the streets through which he walked were as quiet as they were empty. A gentle drizzle was falling. When he reached his destination he was damp and very tired. It was too late for dinner. He ordered some biscuits and a drink. Some members were playing billiards, others were watching them, and making unfavourable comments on their play. A friend came to sit by Willie and talked to him about racing. They had a drink together and then another one. Willie began to feel warm and at ease. The physical well-being spread from his senses to his mind. The regiment had gone but there were still good chaps in the club. The hall-porter came in to warn them that it was nearly closing time. He could not bear the thought of his lonely flat. Was there nowhere they could go on to? he asked. Somebody knew of somewhere—an underground night club, which was sure to be open. They had another drink, and three of them went on. It was far from being a first-class establishment. The jangling music, the tawdry decorations, the tired faces of the girls, brought back to Willie the mood of acute depression from which he had been escaping. Another drink only intensified his gloom. Two of the girls were sitting with them. They knew his companions and they had mutual friends of whom they talked. Willie tried to take part in the conversation, but whatever he said sounded stilted and dull. He wished that Horry were there. Horry always got on with everybody. He knew how to break the ice. Did either of these girls know Horry? Or had they known him, rather, because he was dead, killed in the war. He was an actor but he got killed in the war. Funny thing. He would order another bottle so that they could all drink Horry's health—drink to his memory, rather—no good drinking his health now. Too late. How curious it was that even talking of Horry had helped to break the ice. He was getting on well with the girls now. They were nice girls too, and seemed sympathetic. He had no wish to go home with them, but he needed friends. Why shouldn't a man be friends with girls of that sort? He thought of Felicity and wondered where she was. He knew. She was driving round London, serving her country wherever the bombs were falling thickest. And the regiment was now at sea, going out to the war, hunted by submarines and enemy aircraft. And here was he, sitting half tight in a night club, talking to tarts. 'But it is not my fault,' he muttered to himself, 'God knows it is not my fault.'

Willie had eaten little all that day and, although he had forgotten it, he was very tired, so that the wine was too much for him, and he had to be helped to bed.

When he awoke next morning to a dark December day and found himself in his bleak, ill-kept bachelor flat, with no very clear recollection as to how he had got there, he felt that he had reached the lowest rung on the ladder of depression. There was even a moment when he contemplated putting an end to his life, but he remembered having once heard his father say that to commit suicide was the act of a coward, and therefore, whatever fate might befall him, he knew he must face it rather than run away.

He was disturbed about his behaviour on the previous evening. He was not in the least ashamed of having been drunk, but he remembered talking about Horry, and he was afraid that he might have been maudlin and lachrymose, which he would have considered contemptible. For some time he lay on his back contemplating the misery of human life. Then he rang for breakfast and telephoned to Felicity.

'Willie speaking. Have I woken you up?'

'No, dear idiot, it's just struck eleven.'

'What sort of a night did you have?'

'Pretty foul.'

'Were you up very late?'

'No, the all clear went at 2.30. What were you doing?'

'Well, I stayed up pretty late, and I don't remember hearing the all clear.'

'Tight again, I suppose.'

'I don't see why you need say "again." It happens very seldom. And if it did happen last night, there was good cause for it.'

'Why, what's the matter?'

'You know those chaps I was staying with, up in the north. They have all gone away and they've left me behind again.'

'Oh, my darling!' she cried. 'No wonder, no wonder. What can I do for you?'

'Can you dine with me tonight?'

'I can and will. I have two nights off. I get them every fortnight, you know. I had thought of going to rest in the country, but I hate the country at this time of year. So we'll dine together in that deep underground place in Berkeley Square where you can't hear the bombs, and we'll forget all about the war for once.'

'You're an angel,' said Willie. 'I had just sent out for a pistol to shoot myself. I'll countermand the order and meet you there at eight. I shall be waiting with the largest and coldest martini ever manufactured.'

Having eaten his breakfast and dressed, Willie set forth for his club, fortified in body and soul. He found one of his last night's companions, and eagerly asked him:

'Did I make a fool of myself last night?'

'Not more than usual, old boy.'

'I was feeling a bit depressed and I was afraid I might have got maudlin.'

'I think you asked one of those girls to be a sister to you, and you told the other she reminded you of your mother.'

'I can't have said that,' protested Willie, 'because I never saw my mother.'

'Oh, it may have been your grandmother, but you didn't make any suggestion to either of them that really interested them.'

'No, I know I didn't. I was very tired and I hadn't had any dinner, so I got a bit muzzy, but I remember everything really. It was very good of you to see me home.'

'Oh, I'm glad you remember that,' said his friend–'but it happened to be George who saw you home, and he put you to bed. I felt it my duty to look after those poor girls.'

The chaff that followed made no impression on Willie. His volatile spirit had risen at the thought of dining with Felicity, and looking forward to it made him happy for the rest of the day.

He was first at the rendezvous that evening. He usually was. He ordered double martinis, poured them both into one glass, and ordered another. Then he sat down to wait.

'Hullo Willie,' he heard a voice say. He sprang up gladly to welcome Felicity, and found himself looking at someone whom for a moment he failed to recognise. Then he saw that it was Daisy Summers. They had not met since her elopement. She had changed so much that Willie forgave himself for his delay in recognising her. She had lost her prettiness, but she was still good looking, although her face was hard and lined.

'I am so glad to see you again, Daisy,' he said. 'I'm waiting for someone, but she's always late. Won't you sit down for a minute and have a drink?'

'That's very sweet of you, Willie,' she said. 'You always were very sweet.' She sat down. 'Your girl friend seems to have a healthy thirst, judging from your preparations. I'll have a whisky sour if I may.'

'What's your life now, Daisy? Are you happy?'

'Yes, I'm pretty happy, thanks. I don't think any-body's very happy, do you? I've been working in the postal censorship since the beginning of the war. One feels one's doing something, but it isn't much.'

'And er—your husband?'

'Oh,' she laughed, 'I suppose you mean the Coper. That didn't last long. I've been married since then. I heard from the old skunk the other day. He's living in Ireland, and says it's very nice to be a neutral.'

'He's much too old to fight,' said Willie. 'They tell me that I am, and they won't let me go out.'

'Poor old Willie! You always get the dirty end of the stick; I ought to have married you if I hadn't been a silly little fool, and a bitch. And you never have married, have you? Well, I expect you're wise.' She looked at him reflectively for a moment–'We might go out together one evening.'

'I'd love to,' said Willie, but he didn't sound as though he meant it, so she shrugged her shoulders and said, 'There's my boy. So long, Willie,' and walked over to an overdressed young gentleman who was waiting impatiently at the door.

Willie sat down again and finished his cocktail. 'Poor old Daisy!' he thought. 'She was never a bad sort at heart. She was just fascinated by the Coper. I wonder how it would have turned out if we had married. She seemed to regret it just now. We might have had a lot of children. It would make one feel less useless if one had brought some decent people into the world. It would be interesting to discuss it with her. I might have been more welcoming about her suggestion that we should go out together. I'll go over and speak to her, if only to irritate that young puppy who's with her. Why isn't he in uniform?'

Willie strolled across to where Daisy and her friend were sitting.

'Daisy dear,' he said, 'you suggested our going out together but gave me no address except the postal censorship. What do I do? Ring up the Postmaster-General and say "Please put me through to Daisy"—because I don't know your surname?'

'Silly Willie,' she laughed, while the over-dressed young man glared furiously. 'We're not under the Postmaster-General but the Minister of Information. Here, give me your pencil,' she said to the young man, who sulkily produced a gold one. She scribbled on the back of the menu. 'Here you are,' she said. 'Name, address and telephone number. Mind you don't lose them, and mind you make use of them.'

As Willie returned to his seat, Felicity arrived. 'Who were you talking to?' she asked him.

'An old school friend of yours, Daisy Summers. Do you ever see her now?'

'Never, and I didn't see much of her then. She's made rather a hash of her life, I'm afraid.'

'What has she done?'

'She didn't stay long with that Irishman she ran away with. I doubt if they were ever married, but they pretended to be. Then she did marry somebody quite nice, but it didn't go well, and they separated. Now they say she's being kept by that little Argentine.'

'How dreadful!'

'Oh, I don't know. I dare say she's quite happy.'

'I've promised to go out with her one night.'

'Don't let her seduce you.'

'Would you mind, Felicity, if she did?'

'Not if you promise to tell me all about it.' This hurt Willie. She often hurt him without knowing it.

'Well,' he said, 'if you've quite finished that enormous cocktail and can still walk, we might go over to our table and have some dinner before closing time.'

She had made no comment on the cocktail. This also had disappointed him. He would prepare things to amuse or please her and she would fail to notice them.

As they sat down at their table she said, 'I think it's going to be a bad night. The moon's nearly full and there are no clouds. I'm glad I'm not on duty. By the way, have I seen you since the bombing of London started?'

This was the third unintended blow she dealt him. The dates on which he saw her were engraven on his heart, and the days between impatiently counted.

'Of course you have. We had luncheon together in October, and I saw you for a few minutes when I passed through London last month.'

'Of course,' she said absently, and he knew that she had no memory of those meetings. Then, as though recollecting herself, she turned to him impulsively. 'But tell me about you. They've left you behind. Aren't they devils! I'm sure it's all the fault of that evil Hamilton. But I'm glad I've got you still here—darling. I know I'm selfish.'

All Willie's irritation vanished, forgotten for ever, and he was the happy lover again. So he was able to talk about his disappointment calmly and to discuss the possibilities of invasion, which he had to admit were diminishing. He found that her sympathy really comforted him.

They heard faintly the sound of explosions from time to time, and the head-waiter whispered to Willie that a popular restaurant with a dancing-floor had been struck. He told Felicity, who said, 'Lucky we didn't go there tonight.'

'I wish you could get some more reasonable job,' he said.

'By "more reasonable" you mean safer. I'm beginning to wish so, too. I'm not very brave, you know. And I don't find that I get any braver. It's rather the other way round. I suppose nerves, like everything else, wear out.'

'I heard of a job in the country, near where the regiment was, which might interest you.'

'Oh no,' she said at once, 'I can't leave London. That would be running away. You may think it silly, but that's how I feel—and I think one's own feelings are the best guides one has as to what is right or wrong. I do lots of things that people think wrong, and I don't feel guilty, but if I left London I should be ashamed for the rest of my life.'

'I don't believe you could do wrong,' protested Willie, but she went on without listening to him.

'And I love London so. I think I love it more than England. If you had seen the people of London as I have this month—the ordinary, little, common, heroic people—so brave, so cheerful and so funny—with all their small treasures that they loved blown to smithereens, and making jokes about it, and sticking up their pathetic Union Jacks on heaps of rubble. And the great city itself, with its poor wounded face, so gaunt and ugly and grand and glorious—and old.'

'Yes,' said Willie doubtfully, 'but I like the country better.'

She looked at him, startled, as though she had forgotten he were there. Then she said, slowly:

'My darling Willie. I would not have you any different.'

'Thank you,' he said. 'I so often wish I were different.'

'In what way?' she asked.

'Oh, I should like to be witty and brilliant, as I suppose your other friends are, whom you won't let me see.'

'Talking of brilliance,' she said, 'old Garnet is home again. He's back from North Africa, where he had quite an exciting time. There's nothing brilliant about him. And, oh, Willie, he's grown so old. I can't bear people to grow old, can you? Of course he's more than fifteen years older than me, but he is my brother. I suppose it's the climate of the Far East. He wants so much to see you. I'll give you his telephone number. Write it down, don't lose it and don't get it mixed up with Daisy's, or there might be trouble.'

She gave him the number, which he recorded in his pocket-book, and shortly afterwards they left. As they went up the stairs which led to the street she turned suddenly from the higher step and, bending down, kissed him on the lips.

The streets were quiet now and the moon was bright, but when they came to Jermyn Street they found policemen and firemen guarding the approach. Willie explained that he lived there and was going home. The policeman asked at which number he lived, and on being told said, 'I fear you won't find much of that left, but you can go and have a look. You can't take the car through.' Where had stood the substantial building in which he lived there was an empty space through which the moon, that should have cast a shadow on to the other side of the street, shone without hindrance. From what had been the basement smoke and dust were rising, together with the noise of men at work. Ambulances and fire-engines were standing by.

'Can I be of any help?' asked Willie of somebody who seemed to be in authority.

'No, thanks. The bomb fell an hour and a half ago. We have all the help we need.'

'I lived there,' said Willie, pointing to the void.

'You might very easily have died there tonight,' said the stranger, and Willie, feeling there was no more to be said, returned to the car.

He explained to Felicity what had happened. He had lost everything he possessed in the world, for what he had left in the barracks, that the regiment had recently quitted, had arrived at his flat that day.

'And what are you going to do now, poor Willie?' she asked, smiling at him with amusement and love.

'I've got nowhere to sleep,' he said weakly, standing by the door of the car.

'You had better come and sleep with me,' she said. 'Jump in.'

Half dazed by the sudden event, and still further bewildered by her words, he obeyed her and sat silent by her side while the car sped westwards. It stopped at the entrance that he knew so well.

'Come in,' she said. 'There's nobody here tonight. I'll leave the car here. You can take it in the morning—but you must go early and send it back.'

Willie hardly closed his eyes that night. He had no wish to sleep. He did not want to forget, even for a moment, that Felicity was lying in his arms, and that after all these years she had suddenly given herself to him with the sweetest simplicity and grace. But what did it mean? She had always said she loved him. Did she love him more now, and in a different way? She had always refused to marry him. Surely she would now consent? But what mattered most were the precious moments that were passing. Her head was resting lightly on his shoulder. She slept as silently as a child. He must not wake her. How tenderly he loved her now! Surely this precious night made up for all that he had lost in life.

Long before dawn he left her, very quietly. She turned with a little sigh on to her other side and was still asleep. He was glad that she had not woken. He would not have known what to say. He decided not to take the car, but to walk. He had plenty of time and plenty to think about. As he went down the King's Road, the lurid lamps of night became innocent primroses against the faint morning sky. He felt like a poor man who had suddenly inherited a vast fortune, in which he could hardly believe.

He went first to the site of his flat, in the vague hope of recovering some of his belongings. Any such hope was extinguished by one glance at the scene of devastation. He had then thought to go to his club, having forgotten that it would not be open at that hour. Nor did he like the prospect of arriving in an empty hotel bedroom with nothing but the clothes he wore. Suddenly he remembered that Felicity had given him Garnet's telephone number. Garnet was the type that would not mind being woken before his time. He turned into a telephone booth and rang the number. A voice answered immediately, 'Colonel Osborne speaking.'

'How like Garnet,' thought Willie, 'not to waste time saying "hello."'

'This is Willie Maryngton,' he said. 'Did I wake you up?'

'No, I'm cooking my breakfast.'

'Well, cook some more for me. I've been bombed out, and I'll come along as quick as legs or a taxi can take me.'

'Very well.'

CHAPTER XIV

Garnet's faded eyes shone with pleasure as he opened the door of the flat to Willie.

'Right glad I am to see you,' he said. 'I suppose you got my number from Felicity. I feared she would forget to give it you.'

Then Willie remembered that Garnet was Felicity's brother, and the thought made him feel a little wicked, but very grand.

'I never knew you were such an early bird,' he said, for Garnet was fully dressed, and was laying tea and eggs, toast and marmalade, on the table, all of which he had plainly prepared himself, for there was no sign of a servant.

'I have to be,' he answered–'I'm due at the hospital at nine, and I've patients to see before I go there. I was never so busy in my life.'

'Everyone is except me,' said Willie sadly. 'How right you were to join the R.A.M.C. You've already been to the war, and now you're as useful as you ever were, serving the country every hour of the day, while I, younger than you, am no good for anything.'

He was very hungry, and while they ate their breakfast he recounted to Garnet all his misfortunes.

Garnet listened sympathetically, and at the end said, 'You're looking very tired. I'll prescribe for you. I have a small spare room. You're welcome to live in it as long as you like. Go there now and lie down on the bed and sleep. An old woman comes in the course of the morning to wash up and dust and break the crockery. She won't interfere with you. I'll leave her a note. When you wake the shops will be open. You can go and buy the things you most need. Except breakfast I have no meals here, and never know when or where I may get them, but I shall come back to sleep, and shall look forward to seeing you. Now I must hurry away.'

It was too early, Willie thought, to telephone to Felicity, so he obediently lay down on the bed and slept until past midday. Then it was too late.

He was busy all day buying the things he needed. Every hour he telephoned to Felicity, but there was no reply. He came back to the flat soon after dinner to unpack his purchases, and having done so, was telephoning for the last time when Garnet returned.

'I was ringing up Felicity,' he said, 'but I can get no answer from her flat.'

'She gets a couple of nights off now and then and usually goes away for a rest. She needs it. That work is a high strain on a girl.'

'I am sure it is,' said Willie. 'I wish we could find her something less tiring and nerve-racking.'

'Her health seems satisfactory. You look more tired than she does. What have you been doing all day?'

'Buying my trousseau. I thought it would be fun, but I didn't enjoy it. I suppose I should have made a list before I started. I seem to have got all the wrong things. Look at this beautiful dressing-gown, and I forgot to buy pyjamas and a brush and comb.'

Garnet thought that Willie looked pathetic, helpless and strangely young.

'Come on now,' he said. 'We'll sit down and make a sensible list. I'm used to this sort of thing.'

The next day was Saturday. Willie was due to stay with friends in the country, but he felt he could not leave London without having spoken to Felicity. He believed that she must be wanting to speak to him. She could not know that he was staying with Garnet, but she could have left him a message at the club. It was late in the afternoon when at last he heard her voice on the telephone. He had somehow vaguely expected that it would be altered, fraught with a new intensity, a more intimate affection, but she sounded as she had always done—cheerful and hurried. He told her that he was staying with Garnet, and she approved of the arrangement. He said he had been going away but would stay if she wanted to see him.

'Oh no,' she answered. 'I'll see you when you come back.'

'Which day?'

'You'd better telephone next week.'

He could not leave her so lightly.

'Felicity—' he said.

'What?'

'I'm so glad my flat was bombed.'

'Yes, it must be fun to have the chance of buying every-thing new. I suppose the government will give you the

127

money. Mind you buy some pretty new suits. I'm in a great hurry, have to go on duty, good-bye.'

'Good-bye, my darling Felicity.' She rang off.

Willie felt disappointed, but he did not know why. He had expected something different, but he could not say what. There were moments when he wondered whether the bomb that destroyed his flat had not also scattered his wits, and whether all that had happened afterwards had not been a dream.

It was many days before he saw Felicity again. Small things prevented them from meeting. When they did he came as soon as possible to the point.

'Now will you marry me?' he asked.

'No, my darling,' she answered, 'I won't.'

'But surely what happened the other night has made a difference?'

'I see no reason why it should.'

'But what is it that prevents you from marrying me?'

'It is too difficult to explain.'

'Do you love somebody else more than me?'

She made no reply.

'Do you behave with lots of other people as you have behaved with me?'

'Willie, I refuse to be cross-questioned. You might make me angry, which I have no wish to be. You ought to know me better by now. You love me and you must try to understand me. I know it's hard. I am unreliable. I am wanton. I am ruled by my moods. I suppose that I am very selfish, and that alone would make me a bad wife. But I can't change and I don't want to. You must take me or leave me as I am.'

'But have you no morals?'

'I suppose not. I know that some things are right and some are wrong. Sometimes I do wrong things and I am very sorry, but sometimes I do things which other people think are wrong and which don't seem wrong to me. I thought what we did the other night was not wrong. What did you think?'

'I don't know,' said Willie, which was the truth. He had never asked himself the question, and now he wondered how he could have failed to do so.

'I haven't any religion,' Felicity went on. 'Perhaps I should be better if I had. Mother had none, you know. It was very curious that somebody so conscientious, so conventional and so very good should have been without it.'

They went on to talk about the late Mrs. Osborne, and Willie got no farther in his quest, no nearer to his goal. Despairing of his hopes for marriage, he longed to enquire whether he could expect again what she had given him once. But he dared not ask her, for she still retained some quality—cold, remote and virginal which he trembled to offend.

They separated on that occasion without anything else of importance being said and with the briefest of caresses. The next time they dined he asked her whether her flat was occupied by others that evening. She said that it was. He asked her when it was likely to be empty again. She laughed.

'My poor darling,' she said, 'I know what you mean. But I can't arrange to make love as one fixes dates with dentists. Something will happen—all will be well.'

Their relationship continued with little change. Willie took a furnished flat from a friend for the summer months.

Sometimes his evenings with Felicity would end there, but not often. He never knew how it was to be.

In the autumn he was appointed to the post of instructor in an O.C.T.U. He was jubilant when he got the job, but it proved, in the end, another disappointment. The commandant was only a few years older than Willie, but those few precious years had enabled him to distinguish himself in the first war and earn a row of medals. Willie, on grounds of seniority, was second-in-command, and it just so happened that every one of the junior officers had been out to the war, and had either been wounded or become medically unfit. There was one who had been taken prisoner and had escaped.

Willie was determined not to be sensitive. He fought against it, but he was like a man with some physical blemish at which he feels that others must always be looking. He felt that these young officers must despise him—a dreary old dug-out who had never seen a shot fired in battle. And feeling so, he began to imagine things and to detect sneers where none were intended. He became suspicious and distrustful. He took unreasonable dislikes and began to find pleasure in exerting his authority and snubbing his juniors. He lost the happy gift of inspiring affection which he had unconsciously enjoyed all his life. He was no longer popular, and he knew it.

He came to look forward more and more to his visits to London. There at least he could find at the club the old companions, whom he knew so well, and upon whose good-fellowship he could rely. It never occurred to him that even here the standard had deteriorated; that the worthier members were either serving abroad or working too hard at home to have time for lounging.

Leave was difficult to come by. Although the work was not hard, not nearly so hard as Willie would have liked it to be, he was expected to be always on the spot and to take a sort of schoolmaster's interest in the welfare of the cadets. To go away, even when he had no duties to perform, was frowned upon as showing lack of enthusiasm.

Therefore he saw less of Felicity during this year, and the meetings he had with her were less satisfactory. The friend who had leased him the flat had now reoccupied it, so that he was obliged to stay at hotels, where she would seldom visit him. She also had found some new employment about the nature of which she was extremely reticent. It seemed to occupy more of her time than the previous one, and she was less certain as to when she would be free. Her reticence, combined with her obvious absorption in her work, irritated Willie. He was more easily irritated than he used to be.

Then came a break between two courses at the O.C.T.U. and it brought him a few days' leave, to which he had been looking forward very eagerly. He had made all the preparations for it that men do make when they have time to plan anticipated pleasure. He had made sure of having the rooms he wanted in the hotel he liked best, he had taken tickets for the theatre, he had hired a car for the night, and he had, of course, arranged with Felicity that she should go out with him. When he strode triumphant into his club at midday the hall-porter handed him a folded slip of paper on which was written: 'Miss Osborne telephoned that she was very sorry she would be unable to dine with Captain Maryngton tonight.'

Willie crumpled up the message and, tossing it aside, strode gloomily into the club. He felt that everybody must know, the hall-porter at least must, that he had been let down by a girl, and that he looked like a man waiting with a bunch of violets for someone who never comes. He wondered what he should do with the theatre-tickets as he scanned the welcoming faces of his club-mates, and found none with whom he would care to go to the play. Then he remembered Daisy Summers, and was glad to find that he still had her telephone number. He was pleased and surprised when she answered the call.

'It's Willie speaking,' he said.

'Willie Maryngton?' she asked. 'Come to life again after all these years?'

'It's not so long as you think, Daisy, only about a year. I'm up in London on leave. How about coming out with me, or would it wreck the work of the postal censorship?'

'Silly boy,' she said, 'the postal censorship wrecked me long ago, and now they try to do it without me—and a pretty good mess, I hear, they make of it.'

'But will you come out tonight?'

'Of course I will.'

'Shall we go to a play?'

'If there's anything worth seeing.'

He mentioned the name of the play for which he had got seats.

'You'll never get in there,' she said.

'I'll try—and I'm not so stupid as I used to be, so I'll pick you up at 6.30 and we'll have a good time.'

Daisy was looking very pretty that evening, prettier than Willie remembered, and she was smartly dressed. She was impressed by Willie's efficiency in getting good seats for the most successful play in London, and he saw no need to tell her that he had got them three weeks before. After the theatre they went for dinner to a gay restaurant, where there was music and dancing and where Willie saw several of his friends. Felicity would never go to fashionable places of this kind, but Willie really preferred them. He and Daisy danced together, and drank champagne and he told himself he was having a very good time. They went on to a night club and it was late when he drove her home.

'Come in for a minute and have a drink,' she said.

And he, knowing that it was not to have a drink, accepted the invitation.

He saw Felicity before his leave expired. She made no reference to having thrown him over, until he did. Then she said that she was very sorry, but that it had been quite impossible for her to go out with him that evening. She gave no reason.

'It was of no consequence,' he said. 'I got hold of Daisy Summers and we had quite a good time.' He told her of the play, the restaurant and the night club.

'Did she seduce you?'

'That's a particularly catty way of putting it,' he said.

'You know what I mean.'

'Why should I tell you?'

'Because I want to know, and you know you can trust me.'

'You said you wouldn't mind if she did, so long as I told you.'

'I was wrong. I do mind. I am very sorry.'

'But how do you know what happened?'

'I can't explain how I know,' she answered with a tired sigh, 'but I do. I think you will never be able to deceive me, Willie, and I hope you will never try.'

Willie felt unhappy, not like Lothario, but like a little boy who has been caught doing something of which he is ashamed. He was also full of resentment.

'Why should you make such a fuss?' he protested. 'I thought you attached little importance to such things and didn't think them wrong.'

'Am I making a fuss?' she asked. 'I'm sorry. I know very little about right and wrong, as I've always told you. And I can't see that right and wrong, good and evil, have anything to do with it. I just feel, as I have always felt, that Daisy is not the girl for you. You were very young when you got engaged to her, and you couldn't tell the difference, but you ought to be able to tell the difference now.'

'You hate her, don't you?'

'Good heavens, no! How can you think so? I want her to be happy with her own friends, in her own way.'

'I suppose you think I'm too good for her.'

'No, not that either. She may be better than you, or me, for all I care. But she doesn't suit you, she doesn't become you, and I hate you to do what is unbecoming.'

'I believe you are jealous of her,' said Willie sullenly.

She smiled sadly. 'Perhaps I am; you can think so if you like.'

They parted coldly, as they had never parted before. At the last moment Willie felt inclined to throw himself on his knees and implore her forgiveness. But he was too angry to do so, and he felt strongly that there was no reason why he should. He could not live for ever on the scant charity that Felicity dispensed to him according to her unpredictable moods. Daisy was a jolly good sort. He had no idea what Felicity meant by saying that she didn't become him. He had no wish to understand. Could it be that she was jealous? He would have liked to think it, but he knew that it was not so.

CHAPTER XV

After this the relationship between Willie and Felicity grew less happy. He would still try to see her whenever he came to London, but their evenings together were not as they once had been. The subjects of conversation were no longer the same. Felicity had taken an interest in the regiment, about which Willie had loved to talk. She had come to know intimately the lives and characters of men whom she had never seen, and would often surprise Willie by the accuracy with which she remembered details. She would enquire with real interest about the major's growing family or the subaltern's love affairs. But Willie did not care to talk about the men he was serving with now, or if he did, it was only to recount some remark by one of them, which he had interpreted as a hidden insult. His stories about his brother officers had in the past been full of fun and affection. Now they were laden with malice and dislike.

'Do you know who I met in the street this morning?' he said one evening to Felicity–'that dirty cad Hamilton.'

'I know you don't like him,' she answered, 'but isn't "dirty cad" a bit strong?'

'It's the luck some fellows have that maddens me. I heard he'd been wounded in Africa. It seems to have been pretty bad—his shoulder shattered to pieces, only a few months ago—and here I meet him swanking down Bond Street with his arm in a sling, quite the wounded hero, having just been appointed Military Attaché to one of the few neutral countries where life would be interesting in these days. Why can't they make me a Military Attaché?'

'Perhaps the fact that you can't speak a single word of any foreign language may have something to do with it.'

'I'm told that that doesn't matter a bit. Foreigners respect you all the more if you can't speak their beastly language. I agree with the chap who said that anybody can understand English if spoken loud enough.'

'Really, Willie, you do talk the most terrible nonsense at times.'

Their evenings together seldom ended happily now. Felicity would gently loosen his arms when he threw them around her, and would turn away her face when he wanted to kiss her.

Because he was not happy in his work he was not good at it. He had no gift for teaching and no genuine interest in the progress of those he taught. One autumn evening when the talk had turned on to the fattening of turkeys for the Christmas market, he said, 'That's what our work here is—grooming a lot of silly boys until we think they're fit to be sent out and get killed.' It pleased him to watch the disapproval on the faces of the others, and he did not mind the silence that followed his remark.

He was not surprised therefore when, at the end of the year, his appointment was not renewed, and he found himself once more on the list of elderly officers awaiting employment.

It was now that Willie's friends began to notice a change in him. They found him less good company than he used to be. He had never been a wit or a brilliant conversationalist, but his good manners, his interest in whatever was being said and his happy smile, which came so easily, had made him someone who was welcome wherever he went. His manners were no longer so good, for the fountain from which they sprang, a kind heart, was drying up. He was losing his interest in his fellow beings and finding greater difficulty in smiling. Some thought it was due to an unhappy love affair, others that he was ill, or that he was drinking too much. In fact he was suffering from despair.

He went back to living with Garnet. It saved him the trouble of looking for something else. He disliked taking trouble about anything, and he argued that he might get a new appointment at any moment, so that it was wiser to incur no liabilities. Every morning he would wander to the club and spend most of the day there, doing nothing in particular. Sometimes he would go to a race meeting. More often he would follow the racing results on the tape. Garnet, who watched him with a professional eye, was unhappy about him. He detected symptoms that escaped the eyes of laymen.

'I'm worried about Willie,' he said to Felicity. 'He's letting himself go to pieces.'

'What do you mean?' she asked.

'It is hard to explain, and still harder to understand, unless you have lived in the Far East, as I have. There they say it is the climate which has got you down. There, you know, the retiring age is fifty, and many a man is finished before he reaches it. A moment comes when something happens like the mainspring of a watch breaking. The façade remains the same, perhaps for a long time, and most people can see no difference. I used rather to fancy myself at being able to diagnose this particular disease, and Willie shows symptoms recently that have made me think of it.'

'Oh, Garnet, what can we do to help him?'

'His state may of course be partly due to physical causes. I wanted him to go into hospital for a few days to be overhauled, but he wouldn't hear of it. He said the hospitals were now for fighting soldiers, and he would be ashamed to occupy one minute of a doctor's or a nurse's time.'

'But what can we do to help him?' she repeated.

'A new job that would really interest him, or anything that would take him out of himself would be the best thing.'

'Yes,' she said; 'but he is so hard to place. He isn't very clever, bless his heart, and he has no experience of anything except soldiering.'

'We must think about it,' said Garnet, as he left her. He was, as usual, in a hurry.

There is a district in London, near the heart of it, which has acquired, perhaps undeservedly, a bad reputation. Willie was walking through it one evening. He was returning from the club before dinner, because he had no appetite, and was thinking of going to bed. To his surprise he saw Felicity come out from a block of flats, to which is attached particular notoriety. He thought she looked taken aback when she saw him, but she only laughed when he asked her if that was where she was working now. Two evenings later he was there again, designedly, at about the same hour. Again she came out of the same building, but this time she was not taken aback. She walked up to him and, standing still, said:

'You came here on purpose to spy on me.'

He answered, 'I came here to see if you were really working in that house.'

'Have you nothing better than that to do?' she asked.

'No, by God, I haven't,' he answered passionately, and all her wrath gave way to pity, for she felt as though she had torn the bandage off a festering wound.

She laid a hand on his arm.

'Come into this pub with me, Willie, and have a glass of beer.'

He followed her meekly, and looking round at the unfamiliar precincts he said:

'I don't think I've ever been in an ordinary public-house in London before.'

There was so much of the old, childish Willie in his naïve wonder that she was touched.

'I brought you in here,' she said, 'to give you a lecture, but you're really so touching that I don't think I can.'

'Thank you, Felicity,' he said.

'But listen to me, all the same. You know you are not as nice as you used to be.'

'I know, I know.'

'Do you really think that I'm running a brothel or working in one?'

'How could I think such a thing?'

'Then why did you come here this evening?'

'Perhaps it was just in the hope that I should see you.'

'No, Willie, you know it wasn't. You suspected me. Perhaps you didn't define to yourself what it was that you suspected, but your mind is full of suspicion, hatred and darkness, and it is destroying your heart.'

'I know, I know.'

'You look ill.'

'I feel it. I've felt rotten for days.'

'You ought to be in bed.'

'I stayed there yesterday, but it's so lonely in that grim little room. Garnet's out all day.'

'Well, I'm going to take you there now, and put you to bed, and give you a hot drink and some aspirin. Old Garnet must have a look at you when he comes in. I think you've some fever,' she said, holding his wrist.

She did as she had said, helping him to undress and to get into bed. He was very docile. Before she left him she bent over him and kissed his hot lips with her cool ones, and whispered to him that she loved him still, and that as soon as he was well all should be between them as it had been in the happiest days of the past. His arms held her close to him for a moment, but all he said was 'Alas, alas!'

She scribbled a note to Garnet before she left the flat. He telephoned to her early next morning.

Willie had passed a bad night. He was suffering from pneumonia and had a high fever. But his constitution was good, his heart was sound, there were no complications, no cause for anxiety. Garnet had arranged for a good nurse to look after him. When Felicity went to see him that evening the nurse dissuaded her from going into his room.

He was sleeping, and he needed all the sleep he could get. All efforts to bring down his temperature had failed. His condition was grave. He was no better on the following day. In the evening he fell into a torpor, and early the next morning he died.

CHAPTER XVI

On that day Garnet went to have luncheon at the Service club to which he belonged. He was sad and weary, having sat up half the night. He was overwhelmed with work, and felt that unless he relaxed for an hour and had a quiet meal instead of the glass of milk and sandwiches that he was accustomed to snatch at midday, he would become a casualty himself. That one of the first duties of a soldier was to take care of his own health was a maxim that he frequently impressed on others.

The large club dining-room was nearly full. In a corner he saw an old friend whom he had known in Penang. He was a Scotsman and now, so Garnet noticed, a Brigadier. He sank into the seat opposite, and the two old soldiers began to exchange grievances. Having disposed of the climate, they proceeded to condemn the long hours during which men were expected to work on this side of the world. Garnet explained that this was the first occasion for many months that he had been able to lunch at the club, and that he was only doing so today because he had felt on the verge of a breakdown.

'I was up half the night with a poor fellow who died early this morning, and when I got to the hospital there were a series of operations, so that I haven't even had time to certify his death.'

'Do you have to nurse your patients as well as dose them?' asked the Brigadier.

'No, but this was a dear friend, who had been living in my flat, Willie Maryngton. Did you ever know him?' Garnet mentioned his regiment.

'I think I met him in India—a nice fellow—very sad.'

'Yes indeed, and I suppose I shall have to make all the funeral arrangements.'

'Can't you leave that to his relations?'

'The extraordinary thing is that he hasn't got any. I've known him all my life. His father, who was killed in the last war, made my father his guardian. My father was killed, and Willie was brought up with us from the age of fourteen. He never had a single relation that he knew of.'

The Brigadier seemed interested and began to put questions.

'You say he died this morning? And you have not certified his death? And he had neither kith nor kin?'

Garnet confirmed all these particulars, and the Brigadier went on to make enquiries about Willie's activities during the war, about his age and rank, and ended by asking:

'How many people have you informed of his death?'

'I telephoned to my sister this morning. We were both very fond of him. The nursing sister and the charwoman, who looks after my flat, are of course aware. But why all these questions? It's very kind of you to take so much interest, but I don't quite understand.'

'I am going to ask one more. Did he make a will? If so, where is it? Who benefits by it, and who is the executor?'

'Yes, he made a will. I found it this morning. He left everything to his regimental benevolent fund, and appointed as his executors the firm of lawyers who have always acted for him.'

'Osborne,' said the Scotsman, solemnly, 'do you believe in Providence?'

'No,' said Garnet.

'Well, I do. I was brought up so to believe, and I have never lost my faith. Providence is a great mystery, and I have seen many proofs of it in my life. I am going to make three requests of you. First, that you will not sign that certificate today. Second, that you will not mention Maryngton's death to another living soul. Third, that you will call on me at my office this afternoon.'

Garnet protested that he had no time to spare.

'You will have the time you would have given to registering the death and making the funeral arrangements. You have known me for many years and you know that I do not use words lightly. I tell you that this is a matter of the very greatest importance.'

His Scottish r's rolled impressively, and Garnet, although he felt that he was dreaming, agreed to do as he was asked. Five o'clock was the hour decided upon. The Brigadier drew a blank visiting-card from his pocket book, and wrote upon it. 'That is the address,' he said.

Garnet raised his eyebrows as he read it. 'Well,' he said, 'I should have thought that that was the last place you would have chosen for your office.'

'That,' replied the Brigadier, 'is precisely why I chose it.'

•

They parted, and a few minutes later the Brigadier was entering that ill-famed building outside which Willie had waited a few days before. He took a lift to the third floor, where he let himself into one of the two flats. A slovenly-looking man, sitting in the passage, sprang smartly to attention.

'Fergusson,' said the Brigadier, 'a colonel, R.A.M.C., in uniform, will be calling at five o'clock. Show him straight in. I don't wish to be disturbed while he is with me.'

'Sir,' replied Fergusson.

The Brigadier went into his office, a small room with a large writing-table, sat down and rang the bell. Felicity appeared.

'I shall have a Colonel Osborne coming to see me about five,' he said. 'I don't wish any telephone calls put through while he is here, unless it is a matter of great importance.'

'Colonel Osborne?' she repeated tentatively.

'Colonel Garnet Osborne, R.A.M.C.'

'He is my brother.'

'Is that so, Miss Osborne? Is that so? Another remarkable coincidence. Do you believe in Providence, Miss Osborne?'

'I don't know. I've never thought about it.'

'There are worse things to think about. Your brother is an old friend of mine. We were together in Malaya. Have you all the documents ready and in order for Operation Z?'

'Yes, sir.'

'Have you not thought of any better name for it? Z is a daft sort of a name for an operation.'

'I haven't thought of another.'

'Well, just go on thinking. Thank you.'

She left the room.

When Garnet arrived he was shown straight into the Brigadier, who greeted him with the question:

'Did you know that your sister is my personal assistant?'

'My sister, Felicity?' he asked in astonishment.

'She is Miss Osborne to me, but she tells me you are her brother, and I have no reason to doubt her veracity.'

'Well, well! This is a strange day in my life,' said Garnet.

'And you have not got to the end of it yet,' replied the Brigadier. 'Sit down.'

He then proceeded to confirm all the particulars concerning Willie with which Garnet had supplied him at luncheon. He had a paper in his hand on which he had recorded them. He went through them in order to be sure they were correct.

'Thank you,' he concluded when he came to the end of his questions. 'You have given me some information—and now you are going to receive some in return.

'The purpose of this department, in which you find yourself, Colonel Osborne, is to deceive the enemy. Our methods of deception are, at certain times, extremely elaborate. The more important the military operations under contemplation the more elaborate are our preparations to ensure, not so much that the enemy shall be ignorant of what we intend to do, but rather that he shall have good reason to believe that we intend to do something quite different. I need not impress upon you the importance of secrecy, but I would say to you, what I say to all those who work with me, that there is only one way to keep a secret.

There are not two ways. That way is not to whisper it to a living soul—neither to the wife of your bosom nor to the man you trust most upon earth. I know you for a loyal, trustworthy and discreet soldier, but for a million pounds I would not tell you what I am about to tell you, if I did not need your help.

'A military operation of immense magnitude is in course of preparation. That is a fact of which the enemy are probably aware. Its success must depend largely upon the enemy's ignorance of when and where it will be launched. Every security precaution has been taken to prevent that knowledge from reaching him. Those security precautions are not, I repeat, the business of this department. It is not our business to stop him getting correct information. It is our business to provide him, through sources which will carry conviction of their reliability, with information that is false.

'In a few days from now, Colonel Osborne, the dead body of a British officer will be washed ashore, on the coast of a neutral country, whose relations with the enemy are not quite so neutral as we might wish them to be. It will be found that he is carrying in a packet that is perfectly water-proof, which will be firmly strapped to his chest, under his jacket, documents of a highly confidential character–documents of such vital importance to the conduct of the war that no one will wonder that they should have been entrusted to a special mission and a special messenger. These documents, including a private letter from the Chief of the Imperial General Staff to the General Officer Commanding North Africa, although couched in the most, apparently, guarded language, will yet make perfectly plain to an intelligent reader exactly what the Allies are intending to do. You will appreciate the importance of such an operation; and you will also appreciate that its success or failure must depend entirely upon the convincing character of the evidence, that will prove the authenticity of these documents and will remove from the minds of those who are to study them any suspicion that a trick has been played upon them. The most important of all the links in that chain of evidence must be the dead body on which the documents are found.

'Now, Osborne, you are a medical man, and you must have discovered in your student days, when you were in need of material to work upon, what I have discovered only lately, the extraordinary importance that people attach to what becomes of the dead bodies of their distant relations. People, who can ill afford it, will travel from the north of Scotland to the south of England to assure themselves that the mortal remains of a distant cousin have been decently committed to the earth. You can hardly imagine the difficulty I have experienced. The old profession of body-snatching has no longer any practitioners, or I would have employed one. I have now secured the services of a gentleman in your line of business, a civilian, and our hopes rest upon what a pauper lunatic asylum may produce. But there must be difficulties. You may have heard, Osborne, that death is the great leveller, but even after death has done his damnedest there is apt to remain a very considerable difference between a pauper lunatic deceased from natural causes and a British officer, in the prime of life, fit to be entrusted with a most important mission.'

'I see what you are getting at,' interrupted Garnet. 'You want me to agree to poor Maryngton's body being used for this purpose.'

'Bide a while, bide a while,' said the Brigadier, who had not completed his thesis. 'You will appreciate the cosmic importance of this operation, upon which the lives of thousands of men must depend, and which may affect even the final issue of the war. This morning I was wrestling desperately with the problem of the pauper lunatic for whom an identity, a name, a background had to be created. Our enemies are extremely painstaking and thorough in their work. You may be quite certain that they have copies of the last published Army List, and I am sure that they have also, easily available, a complete register of all officers who have been killed since that publication, or whose names have appeared in the obituary columns. Their first action on being informed that the body of a dead British officer has been discovered will be to ascertain whether such a British officer was ever alive. If they fail to find the name of such an officer in the Army List their suspicions will be aroused, and those suspicions, once aroused, may easily lead them to the true solution of the mystery. We should be forced to give to our unknown one of those names that are shared by hundreds, and should have to hope that, in despair of satisfying themselves as to the identity of the particular Major Smith or Brown in question, they would abandon the enquiry. But—I say again—we are dealing with a nation whose thoroughness in small matters of detail is unequalled, and it is my belief that within a few days the chief of their intelligence service would be informed that no officer of the name in question has ever served in the British Army. From that moment all the information contained in the documents, about which I told you, would be treated as information of doubtful value and of secondary importance. The result might well be that the whole operation would fail completely.

'While this grave problem is occupying my mind today, you sit yourself down before me and tell me of an officer who died this morning, whose death has not been registered, who has no relations, who was of an age and standing entirely suitable for such a mission and over the disposal of whose dead body you have control. Call it the long arm of coincidence, whatever that may mean, if you desire, but to me, Colonel Osborne,' the Brigadier's voice grew hoarse with emotion, 'it is the hand of Providence stretched out to aid His people in their dire need, and I ask you to give me your help, as God has given me His, in the fulfilment of my task.'

He ceased and both sat silent. After a while Garnet said:

'What you are asking me to do is very extraordinary, and although I perfectly understand the terrible urgency, you must allow me to reflect.' He paused—and then continued: 'In the first place I should be acting quite illegally. I have no more right to conceal Maryngton's death than I have to dispose of his body.'

'*Silent leges inter tirma*,' replied the Brigadier. 'I will give you my personal guarantee, written if you wish it, that will cover you from any legal consequences.'

They sat again in silence for two or three minutes. When Garnet next spoke it was to ask:

'What should I actually have to do? And what am I going to say when Maryngton's friends, many of whom must have known that he was living with me, ask me what has become of him?'

The Brigadier was obviously relieved. He felt now that the other's mind was moving in the right direction.

'What you have to do is to lay out by the side of Maryngton's body tonight his uniform, omitting no detail of it. Don't forget his cap or his belt, and above all make sure that the identity disc is there. Put on the table his watch, his cheque-book and any small personal possessions that he always carried. At 2 a.m. some friends of mine will call upon you. There may be two of them, there may be three. You will show them which is Maryngton's room. Then you will go to bed and sleep soundly. You will, however, dream that Maryngton comes to you in the night and tells you that he is leaving England in the early morning. His mission is of a secret nature, and in case anything should go wrong he hands you his will, which you have already told me is in your possession. When you wake in the morning he will certainly have gone, and you will therefore believe your dream was a reality. It will probably be many days before you have to answer any enquiry. During those days you will repeat to yourself continually how he told you one night that he was leaving on a secret mission, how he gave you his will, and how he was gone on the following morning. You will come to believe this yourself, and it will be all that you know, all that you have to say to anyone who asks questions. One day you will read in the paper that Maryngton has died on active service. Then you will send his will to his lawyers; and that will be all.'

Again Garnet sat in silence for several minutes.

'Does my sister know about this affair?' he asked.

'Miss Osborne is aware,' said the Brigadier, 'that an operation of this nature is in preparation.'

'I would rather,' said Garnet, 'that she did not know that it was—that we were making use of—damn it, respect for the dead bodies of those we love is a very profound instinct in human nature. Willie Maryngton has been like a brother to us all our lives. I am sure it would distress her horribly.'

The Brigadier looked grave and answered:

'You may be sure that I have already given very careful consideration to this part of the problem. Besides ourselves there are three other people, so far as we are aware, who know that Maryngton died of pneumonia this morning. I have decided that the best method of securing the discretion of the nurse and the servant is to say no more to them on the subject. To neither of them will the case present any peculiar or interesting feature. To impose secrecy upon them would merely stimulate their curiosity. If either of them reads the announcement of his death, which is unlikely, the fact that it is described as having taken place on active service will be accepted as part of the incomprehensible vocabulary of Whitehall.

'Now your sister is another matter. I have the greatest confidence in her reliability, but I cannot expect even her to keep a secret if she doesn't know it is a secret. She may have told someone of Maryngton's death already. If not, she is almost sure to do so.'

'She's a strange girl,' said Garnet; 'she keeps her friends in separate compartments, isolated cells as it were. Since my brother was killed she and Willie had no mutual friends. I think it unlikely that she has told anybody. But I can make sure, which I promise to do. What is more, I can pretend to her that my conduct has not been strictly professional in allowing a friend to die in my own flat without calling in a second opinion, and failing to inform the authorities within twenty-four hours. On that ground I can ask her not to mention the matter, and then we can safely count on her silence.'

'I don't like it, Osborne,' said the Brigadier. 'In affairs of this sort I like to have everything water-tight. The smallest leak may sink the ship—and what a ship it is! Think, man, the whole British Empire is on board!'

An ugly cloud of obstinacy crept into Garnet's eyes.

'I'm sorry,' he said. 'The whole business is hateful to me, and I just can't bear to bring my sister into it. Between ourselves, I once suspected that she was in love with Maryngton. I even hoped that they might marry. Can you imagine telling a girl what it is that you are intending to do with the dead body of a man who might have been her husband? It is a kind of sacrilege.'

The Brigadier looked into Garnet's eyes, and he saw the obstinacy that lay there. He looked at his watch, and then he said,

'I'll not tell her. You have my word for it.'

Garnet sighed.

'In that case I suppose I must consent,' he said. 'I can see no good reason for not doing so—except sentiment, or perhaps sentimentality—and I have never considered myself to be ruled by either. In any case, service must come first. You have given me my instructions. They are simple enough. They shall be carried out. Have you anything further to ask of me?'

'Lay out the uniform,' said the Brigadier, omitting no detail of it. 'Leave the small personal possessions on the table. Open the door when the bell rings. Dream as I told you, and believe that your dream is true.'

They shook hands and Garnet turned to go.

'One more detail,' said the Brigadier. 'You have not by any chance got some spare major's badges among your equipment?'

'I doubt it,' said Garnet.

'Very well. My friends will provide them. I have been thinking that the rank of captain is just one too low for an officer charged with such a very important mission. He appears as a captain in the last pre-war Army List. If he had been employed on important work since then he would have become a major by now, so I intend to make him one. These small details can prove of vast importance in this sort of work.'

'Oh dear,' said Garnet, 'that was the promotion he was so anxious to obtain. Poor Willie! It is a heartbreaking business.'

'Ay,' said the Brigadier. 'Operation Heartbreak would not be a bad name for it.'

Felicity met Garnet in the passage. 'Come into my room,' she said. 'I've got a cup of tea for you.'

'It will be welcome,' he answered. 'I had a wretched night and I've been hard at it all day. Odd to find you here. You are, I must say, a very secretive girl.'

'Now tell me all there is to tell about Willie. I felt that I couldn't bear to hear more this morning, when you told me he was dead, so I rang off in an abrupt and what must have appeared a callous way. But I can bear it now. Go on.'

Garnet recounted the course of the short illness and explained that it was not uncommon for healthy men in middle-age to be carried off suddenly by a sharp attack of pneumonia.

'But I do think,' he went on, 'that there was something else, another contributory cause as it were, in Willie's case. I told you not long ago that I thought there was something wrong with him. In all illness, and especially in cases of this sort, the will of the patient plays a great part. There comes a moment when an effort is required. In this case that effort wasn't made. I am afraid that one of the reasons why Willie died was that he did not greatly wish to live.'

'Ah!' Felicity gave a little cry, as though in sudden pain, but said no more.

After a pause Garnet went on to ask:

'Do you happen to have mentioned his death to anyone you've seen today, Felicity?'

'No,' she answered. 'I haven't seen anyone, for one thing, and there isn't anyone to whom I talk about Willie, for another.'

'Well, I had rather that you kept it to yourself,' he said, and went on to tell her the story he had invented about his alleged lapse from professional rectitude.

'I promise not to breathe a word,' she said, but she looked at him with curiosity, asking herself whether such conduct was really unprofessional and, if so, whether Garnet could have been guilty of it.

'How about the funeral?' she asked.

'Oh, it seems there are some distant cousins in Yorkshire. The lawyers have communicated with them. They want him to be buried up there. It appears his forbears came from that part of the country. I couldn't object.'

'He always told me he hadn't any cousins anywhere, but I'm glad they've been discovered. I hate funerals, and he would never have expected me to go to Yorkshire to attend one among people whom I don't know.'

Hers was not an inquisitive nature, but it seemed strange to her that cousins who had remained unknown throughout his life should assert themselves within a few hours of his death.

Having finished his tea, Garnet rose to go.

'Good-bye, dear old Garnet,' she said. 'Now that you have found out where I work you might come and see me sometimes. I can always give you tea.'

'I should like to come,' he replied. 'I am very busy, but I feel lonely sometimes.'

'I suppose everybody does.'

'Yes, I suppose so.'

He went, and a few minutes later the bell summoned her to the Brigadier. She picked up her pad and pencil and went into his room.

'I had an interesting conversation with your brother,' he said. 'Did he tell you about it?'

'No.'

'I told you that I met him in the Far East. We both know something about the pretty ways of the Japanese and we've been having a fine crack about them. Our Government will never resort to bacteriological warfare, you know, but I think it's just the sort of trick the Japs might play on us. So I was thinking that we might get it whispered around that we had something up our sleeve in that line more terrible than anything they would imagine. That might make them think twice before they used it.'

'It might, on the other hand, make them use it immediately so as to be sure of getting their blow in first.'

'Ay, but I think they've held off poison gas so far because they suspect we've got a deadlier brew than they have. Your brother is very knowledgeable in the matter of oriental diseases.'

Felicity wondered why he was telling her all this. She had studied the Brigadier's methods, and she had noticed that when he volunteered information it was usually with a motive, and that the information itself was usually incorrect. Was he trying to deceive her, or had he perhaps some more subtle purpose?

'To change the subject,' he went on, 'to Operation Z, or Operation Heartbreak, as I'm thinking of calling it. I've received information from that doctor of whom I told you. He has to hand exactly what we were looking for. So the matter is now urgent. Time and tide—we depend on both of them, and neither will wait upon the other. There is not an hour to be lost. The Admiralty are standing by. They await only the pressure of a button to go ahead. And I am about to press that button. You have the wallet and the papers. I should like to have another look at them.'

As Felicity went to her room to fetch them it occurred to her that the news which had come to the Brigadier from the doctor could not have been received that afternoon by telephone, for she had had control of all the calls that reached him, and it was strange, if time were precious, that he should have wasted so much of it in discussing remote possibilities with Garnet, and should have attached so much importance to the conversation.

She returned with the carefully constructed waterproof wallet and a thin sheaf of papers. The Brigadier slipped on a pair of gloves before he touched them. She smiled.

'You think, Miss Osborne, my precautions are a wee bit ridiculous. But it is always wiser to err on the side of prudence. I hope that in a few days these papers will be in the hands of a gentleman as prudent as I am, and better equipped. It may be that he will have them tested for finger-prints, and it may be that he has a photograph of my finger-prints on his writing-table. We are dealing with a very thorough people, Miss Osborne, a very thorough people.

'So this is the letter from the C.I.G.S.,' he went on, carefully taking it out of the envelope. He read it slowly and chuckled. 'He must have enjoyed putting in that joke about the Secretary of State. It just gives the hallmark of authenticity. He has made a very good job of it indeed.'

He laid the papers on the table in front of him, and remained silent for three or four minutes, apparently lost in thought.

'A man setting out on a journey of this sort,' he said at last, speaking very slowly, 'would probably put into his wallet what was most precious and dear to him. A married man might put there the photographs of his wife and children. This is to be a single man.' He paused again. 'Do you think, Miss Osborne,' he asked, 'that you could draft a love letter?'

'I can try,' she replied, impassively.

'Do that,' he said. 'Meanwhile I must get on to the Admiralty and see the young men in our Operations Branch, who have a full night before them.'

She rose to go.

'Make sure that there's no "G.R." in the corner of the paper you write on, nor "For the service of His Majesty's Government" in the watermark.'

'I will make sure,' she said.

'And there is one more thing.' He hesitated. 'You must try to make that letter the kind a man would think worth keeping.'

'I will try,' she said, and left the room.

The Brigadier continued to look at the door after she had shut it. He had the habit of observing people closely. Was he mistaken or had he detected a light of revelation in her eyes, a kind of exultation in her manner, the air of one who goes with confidence to the performance of a grateful task?

He had no time to waste on speculation. His evening was fully occupied. He first had a long interview with two young men, who were members of his staff but not regular attendants at the office. Then there were a number of telephone conversations with the Admiralty and with other government departments. When he looked at his watch he was surprised to see how late it was. He rang the bell and Felicity came in with a sheet of paper in her hand.

'I am sorry I have detained you so long,' he said–'all our preparations are now complete. Have you drafted the letter that I suggested?'

She handed him the paper she was carrying and said nothing. He put on his gloves before taking it and held it up to the light, examining it with a magnifying glass, and then, seemingly satisfied with his inspection, adjusted his spectacles and began to read:

Darling, my darling, you are going away from me and I have never told you how much I love you. How sad, how heartbreaking it would be if you had never known. But this will tell you, and this you must take with you on your dark mission. It brings you my passionate and deathless love. Forgive me all the disappointment that I caused you. Remember now only the hours that I lay in your arms. I cannot have known how much I loved you until I knew that you must go away. I have been weak and wanton, as I warned you once that I should always be, but I have been in my own odd way, believe me, oh believe me, darling, I have been true. When we meet again you will understand everything and perhaps we shall be happy at last.

When he had finished reading it he did not look up.
'This should be signed with a Christian name,' he said.
'Have you any suggestions?' she asked. There was a faint note of bitterness in her voice.
'An unusual one is likely to be more convincing than a common one. Your brother told me yours this afternoon. Have you any objection to making use of it? People show by the way they sign their own names that they are

accustomed to doing so. Handwriting experts might be able to tell the difference.'

'I will sign it "Felicity,"' she said.

'If the pen you have in your hand is the one with which you wrote the letter,' he said, 'you can sign it here,' and he pointed to the chair on the other side of his table. She sat down and wrote and handed him back the letter. At the end of it she had written in her clear, bold hand "Felicity" and at the beginning "My Willie."

The Brigadier made sure that the ink was dry and then he crumpled the letter between his two hands so that she thought he was going to throw it into the waste-paper basket. He smoothed it out again very carefully, saying as he did so: 'This is a letter which a man would have read many times. It should bear signs of usage.' Then, still looking down at the letter and still smoothing it, he said:

'So you have guessed our secret. I gave your brother my word of honour that I would not tell you. I think I have kept my word.'

'But why did he want me not to know?' she asked.

'He feared that it would cause you pain.'

'He ought to have understood,' she said, 'that it is what Willie would have wished more than anything in all the world.'

CHAPTER XVII

Dawn had not broken, but was about to do so, when the submarine came to the surface. The crew were thankful to breathe the cool, fresh air, and they were still more thankful to be rid of their cargo. The wrappings were removed, and the Lieutenant stood to attention and saluted as they laid the body of the officer in uniform as gently as possible on the face of the waters. A light breeze was blowing shoreward, and the tide was running in the same direction. So Willie went to the war at last, the insignia of field rank on his shoulders, and a letter from his beloved lying close to his quiet heart.

EPILOGUE

Everything worked as had been intended. The neutral government behaved with the courtesy that is expected of neutral governments. After a certain delay, such as is inevitable in the movements of government departments, they informed the Ambassador, with regret, that the body of a British officer, whose identity appeared to be established, had been washed up by the sea, and that he was bearing a waterproof packet which they had the honour to forward intact. They would be glad to make any arrangements for the funeral that His Excellency might desire. They did not think it necessary to mention that the packet in question had been already opened with infinite care, and that before being closed again with care as infinite, every document in it had been photographed, and that those photographs were now lying under the eyes of the enemy, where the false information that they contained powerfully contributed to the success of one of the greatest surprises ever achieved in military history.

•

And so it was that the Military Attaché, the Assistant Military Attaché and the Chaplain found themselves travelling from the capital to the coast on that hot morning.

AFTERWORD

Alfred Duff Cooper (1890–1953)—the "Alfred" is silent—
is an example of a type the British used once to produce
in far greater quantities than now, when he has practically
become extinct: the "all-rounder." You could put them
anywhere, set them any task, and they would perform,
sometimes brilliantly, sometimes merely capably, rarely
catastrophically, usually distinctively. There was a spirit of
fun, of amateurism, of sport, in what they did. The Battle
of Waterloo was won, supposedly, "on the playing fields of
Eton." The famous/notorious Victorian poem "Vitaï Lam-
pada" ("Play up! play up! and play the game!") by Sir Henry
Newbolt has cricket in its first stanza, colonial warfare in
its second, and a conclusion in its third. The three things
are continuous, co-extensive, inevitable, irresistible. The
Antipodean Clive James—a lifelong student of English
frailty and himself something of an all-rounder—jeered:
"It is not easy, at this distance, to be sure of what it was that
Duff Cooper actually *did*," but this is exactly the point.
The style is greater than the man, and the man is greater
than his CV.

So much of what one thinks of as Britishness—or, as I would say, that *used* to be Britishness—is invested in that type: anti-professionalism, unpreparedness, improvisation, flippancy, grace under pressure (Hemingway's definition of courage), pleasantness, wit. You wouldn't know what they were going to say—heck, they might themselves not know what they were going to say—but you would turn out to hear them speak, in Parliament, on the hustings, at the club. It was all rather eighteenth century, rather personal, rather C. J. Fox, that world of "brilliant success without undue application." Along with a feeling of mild disdain for public work, a condescension towards duty, and an unhesitating patriotism, went an ironic acceptance that one's very best offerings would evaporate in a puff of wit in front of a handful of witnesses generally the worse for wear. Duff Cooper's very good biographer, the historian John Charmley, laments that there is no way of doing justice to the reported brilliance of Duff Cooper's conversation in small intimate groups of friends. "A Pierrot of the moment," was someone's beautiful description of the man and the ethos. This too is part of the type. There is almost something Nietzschean—and hence unexpectedly Continental—about them, an inversion of values, so that the permanent is temporary, the temporary is permanent, the serious is silly, and having fun is what matters. They *expected* to be in over their heads, but they fought and won two world wars and carried an empire for a few hundred years. Their descendants no longer seem capable of running a country. And, moving on to serious matters, it's hard to think of any British cabinet minister in the last thirty, even fifty years, from whom one would care to commission a novel. (Answers on a postcard, please.)

Duff Cooper, then: soldier, diplomat, parliamentarian, cabinet minister, man of letters. Also gambler, lover, and bon viveur. He came from a family flecked with elopements and illegitimacies, though also ("a dash of Hanoverian blood") with ancestral ties to the British royal family; Lady Erroll, his great-grandmother, "was one of the brood of nine FitzClarences who were the offspring of the liaison between the future William IV and the actress Mrs. Jordan." Duff Cooper was a product of Eton and New College, Oxford; a war hero, in what appears to have been a somewhat chaotic solitary action in the so-called "Battle of the Mist" on the Albert Canal, for which he received a DSO; and a celebrity husband as the successful wooer of a famous British beauty, Lady Diana Cooper, all by 1920. Restored to civilian life, he first occupied a niche in the Foreign Office before entering politics. He was a conservative member of parliament for twenty years, later a junior minister in the War Office, then First Lord of the Admiralty. Constants in his thinking—and, unlike too many of his successors, he *did* think—were a suspicion of Russia and Germany, a sense of the coming war, a deep Francophilia, and an espousal, ultimately, of Western European union as the only guarantee of continued British independence. (Brexit would have horrified him, as it would Churchill.)

He resigned in protest at Neville Chamberlain's appeasement policy, then returned to government under Churchill as a somewhat redundant and ill-defined Minister of Information (it's hard to say whether he was for or against). Churchill also sent him on special errands to Indonesia in 1942 and Algiers in 1944. His apotheosis and his last detail came as His Majesty's ambassador to France, where the post-1945 Labour government left him in post for another couple of years, in token of what were perceived to be his close ties to the country and to de Gaulle. When he was let go, he accepted the title of Viscount Norwich ("a little Norwich is a dangerous thing," he liked to quip), bought a ravishing little chateau in Chantilly, took a job on the board of the International Wagons-Lits, and was an early tax exile, twenty years before the Rolling Stones. Having written well-received books earlier on Talleyrand, on Field Marshal Earl Haig, on the biblical King David, and on the young Shakespeare, he published his one novel, *Operation Heartbreak* in 1950. His brisk and entertaining memoir *Old Men Forget* came out in 1953, just before he died, on New Year's Day 1954, on a cruise liner on the way to the West Indies, for his health. John Charmley writes: "Few men can have enjoyed life more than Duff."

Operation Heartbreak is as creditable, as surprising, as abundantly and elegantly good, as anything else Duff Cooper turned his mind and hand to. While I don't believe that everyone has a novel inside them, this one is well worth rediscovering and makes me wish its author had written more of the things. It has a keen sense of shape and pace, coaxes an effortless and uncoercive plot out of Garnet and Horry, Felicity and Daisy, Hamilton and Maryngton, and ends most if not all its chapters with a sonorous droop. Duff Cooper manages his mostly short, often ironic, and sometimes profound sentences with the purposeful dexterity of a croupier raking in the errant tokens:

> Horatio, Mrs. Osborne's second son, was nothing so serious, or so foolish, as a pacifist.

> 'Here, give me your pencil,' she said to the young man, who sulkily produced a gold one.

> But, because men can never be quite happy for long, he suffered during these years from one continual source of irritation and experienced one great sorrow.

> Self-consciousness, the curse of English youth, fell from them, and they found words coming to them easily.

It is a book with information, even wisdom, to burn: that spilt champagne should be dabbed behind the ears; that something happens to men at fifty; that a promotion to the rank of major can be called getting a majority (and Felicity got her name because she was born the day her father came into one); that Scots make the best spymasters. The eponymous "Operation Heartbreak" is based on the historical "Operation Mincemeat" from 1943—which would have come under his auspices when Duff Cooper was Minister of Information. The corpse of a dead British officer, one Major Martin, was dropped in the Mediterranean by a British submarine, expressly for the enemy to find. Sealed in waterproofed covers he was carrying top-secret documents relating to an imminent British attack on Yugoslavia. The documents were false, a classic piece of British misdirection; the operation worked a treat; and the British and Americans met with far less resistance when they—in fact—invaded Sicily instead. The post-War British government, addicted like most governments, even in those more innocent times, to secrecy, was unhappy to have the operation put in a novel; it's as well their efforts to suppress the book failed.

But this, if you like, is a diversion, the book's trick ending, a redemptive play on the uses of uselessness, a burst of posthumous heroism. It only gets going in the last twenty pages, when the hero—or anti-hero?—is dead. There is a case for saying that there was another "Operation Heartbreak," sustained not for a few weeks but for over forty years, every bit as successful, whose object was not the Axis powers, but the "man who never was," Willie Maryngton. It was mounted—intentionally, unintentionally, implacably, it hardly matters—by the society that taught him to talk to men but not women, and to ride horses but not drive tanks; by the family that was not his but in which he grew up; by the army that did not want to make true use of him; and by the women who, even after being kissed, respectively slept with, did not think to marry him. This is the other, perhaps the true "Operation Heartbreak." A social comedy of manners that is radiant with loneliness. The story of someone who qualifies for his posthumous heroism by the utter lack of connections he is born into; an orphan gifted with just enough insight to see himself as "a soldier who never went to war, and a lover who never lay with his mistress."

Yes, Willie Maryngton is a kind of cipher, a man with no blood ties, no successes, and no real abilities, a man without qualities except for a temporary popularity which wears out as he ages into disappointment, as old as the century in which he feels entirely wrong. He works both as a twentieth century phenotype, not far from those of left-wing writers, the Winston Smith of George Orwell's *Nineteen Eighty-Four*, or the Diederich Hessling of Heinrich Mann's *Der Untertan*, and a representative British character, struggling with the immemorial British difficulties, all to do with deviousness and indirectness and frankness: the difficulty of speech, the difficulty of comprehending the speech of others, the difficulty of dissembling, the difficulty of sincerity, the difficulty of finding a subject. The failure to speak unambiguously ("This was not quite what Felicity had meant") is matched in this book only by the failure to understand ("So Willie's conversation with Horry ended, as had his conversation with Garnet, with a remark that he couldn't understand"). Clarity, at such moments when it comes—Hamilton's, Felicity's—is only ever destructive. It is something much more to be feared than sought after.

It is perhaps a little astonishing that a man so blessed with talent and facility as Duff Cooper should have been granted such insight into the predicament of his tongue-tied and monoglot and club-bound countrymen, and one wouldn't look nowadays for any such empathy or analysis. But as the late critic John Bayley nobly surmised in an essay on Duff Cooper in the *London Review of Books*: "Successful people often understand unusually well the true nature of disappointment and failure, for it is implicit in their success, and it is this realisation which moves in the background of the short novel. Perhaps to have done brilliantly and achieved much, but not quite so much as some people professed to have thought you would, is harder than to fail."

In 1953, a couple of years after *Operation Heartbreak*, another writer, enabled by the shattering success of his new project to move to those West Indies that Duff Cooper set sail for but failed to reach alive, came up with a different phenotype of British hero, and the all-action Etonian James Bond was launched by Ian Fleming in a book called *Casino Royale*. At which point, threescore and ten years ago, one might say the British finally and irrevocably parted company with the reality that is so gently and persistently and compassionately adumbrated in *Operation Heartbreak*— and with it the qualities of sadness and sympathy and mortality and thoughtfulness—and entered the garish and straightforward new world of violent fantasy.

Michael Hofmann
Gainesville, FL, 2023

McNally Editions reissues books that are not widely known but have stood the test of time, that remain as singular and engaging as when they were written. Available in the US wherever books are sold or by subscription from mcnallyeditions.com.